A QUARTERLY SCIENCE FICTION & FANTASY MAGAZINE

ISSUE #3 | SUMMER 2017

TABLE OF CONTENTS

MYTHIC
A Quarterly Science Fiction & Fantasy Magazine
ISSUE # 3 SUMMER 2017

Published by Founders House Publishing LLC

MYTHIC: A Quarterly Science Fiction & Fantasy Magazine
is a project and publication of Founders House Publishing LLC.

www.mythicmag.com

www.foundershousepublishing.com

ISBN 13: 978-945810-07-7
ISBN 10: 1-945810-07-6

Printed in the United States of America

MYTHIC is quarterly magazine published by Founders House Publishing LLC. We publish speculative fiction, specifically science fiction and fantasy. Our mission is to expand the range of what is currently possible within both genres. We like new perspectives and new spins on familiar tropes. Diversity is a hallmark of our vision.

One year, four-issue subscriptions to *MYTHIC* cost *$40*. You can subscribe by visiting www.mythicmag.com or make out checks to Founders House Publishing and send them to the following address: 614 Wayne Street, Suite 200A / Danville, IL 61832

If you are interested in submitting to *MYTHIC*, you can visit our website for information regarding our submission guidelines.

www.mythicmag.com/submissions.html

MYTHIC: A QUARTERLY SCIENCE FICTION & FANTASY MAGAZINE

EDITED AND DESIGNED BY
SHAUN KILGORE

———

SPECIAL THANKS TO JOHN MICHAEL GREER

SPECIAL THANKS TO OUR SUBSCRIBERS AND PATRONS ON PATREON:

YOU HELP MAKE MYTHIC
BETTER ONE ISSUE AT A TIME.

(www.patreon.com/mythicmag)

Coming Next Issue in *MYTHIC*

INTRODUCTION
EDITING FUN

BY SHAUN KILGORE

Dear Readers, MYTHIC is back again with its third issue and I've included a slew of great new stories. Serious and even dark fantasies mingle with more humorous tales. There is so much potential in science fiction and fantasy and the writers are certainly exploring them, and stretching the boundaries. I hope to keep seeing that from those of you who've submitted work. That's why MYTHIC exists, after all. I love variety and each issue strives for that if nothing else.

The pendulum will swing back and forth between the broader categories of science fiction and fantasy every quarter. There might be more of one than the other in a given issue but that will change.

I'm having fun. Being an editor can be lots of fun but it is challenging. Good stories multiply fast in the submissions and it takes care to choose the stories that will appear in these pages. As always, I thank the writers for their in-terest in MYTHIC and for their contributions.

With the limited budget this publication has, I've been fortunate to receive the support of writers and readers alike who believe in what I'm doing.

But I want to keep going. I want to keep this magazine coming to you so I'm asking you to share MYTHIC with others. Buy a subscription if you haven't already. Support us in some other way, such as Patreon. We would like to keep building and increasing our readership.

Thanks again for reading. I hope you enjoy MYTHIC #3!

Interested in submitting stories to MYTHIC? E-submissions may be sent to **submissions@mythicmag.com**. For complete guidelines, visit us at: **www.mythicmag.com**

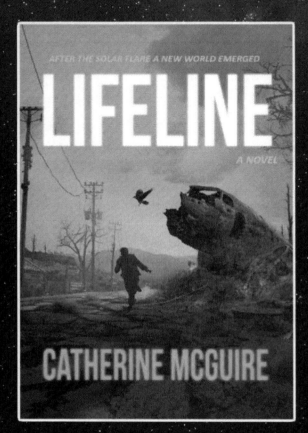

ZAWADI'S CHOICE

BY D.A. D'AMICO

The world had been a much simpler place before Nimit. Zawadi had her sisters, her city and the villages surrounding it. The sun had hung motionless in the sky, fading into night, brightening into day, and she'd never given a moment's thought to who'd built it all, or what lay beyond the Endless Forest. Now, the world had been revealed as artificial, thousands of generations old and vast beyond imagining. It was an eggshell, with the sun as its yolk, the sky its albumen, and Zawadi smaller than the smallest imaginable speck.

"I know all too well what it's like to feel overwhelmed," Nimit said as if reading her thoughts. Zawadi remained silent. Overwhelmed didn't begin to explain her feelings.

Across the cabin, a little girl wouldn't stop crying. She fidgeted, climbing over silver trimmed couches and under low teak tables. It drove the man standing beside her crazy, and he huffed as he rearranged the bloated orange balloon of his suit.

"Hold her still." He glared at the woman beside him, his voice like gravel striking glass.

"She's scared, Devon."

"She's a child, Matti. He grabbed the girl, sitting her firmly on her mother's lap where she belonged. "That's how you handle an unruly child."

The woman rolled her eyes.

Zawadi grinned. It was the first normal thing she'd seen since Nimit had come to take her away. This family of merchants, a quartet of diplomats, and two technological advisors were her last connection with home. It tempered her excitement, but she finally had her chance to say goodbye to the smothering seclusion of her father's court.

"Find something funny?" Nimit, the eunuch who'd soon be her spouse, brushed a tangle of dark curls from his eyes and clasped jeweled-covered fingers across his slender waist. His smile seemed genuine as he turned from his conversation with a short, beak-nosed technologist with greying hair and nut-brown skin.

"It's nothing." Zawadi looked away, nervously twisting the braided silk that hung over her bare left shoulder.

The four elaborately painted scarves had been a gift from her father, and she wore them wound tightly into a cap over her shaved head. It was her wedding costume, and the reason for her anxiety.

"No... Don't let that smile escape." He clucked, his breath smelling of ginger and mint. His soft accent made his words seem squeaky. "It's so much better than the look of doom you've worn all day."

She forced another smile. Nimit frowned, pouting. "You can do better than that."

"I could." She dropped her gaze. "But then where would the challenge be?"

Nimit laughed so loud heads turned. The hawk-faced technologist scowled as if Zawadi were somehow corrupting their host, and she decided then and there she liked Nimit.

Tenuous shimmers gave her only the barest sensation of movement, as if their craft rested in the center of a gentle river. It was difficult to imagine they were already traveling at many times the speed of sound, and it would take a week of such travel to reach Nimit's home city. It was a baffling expanse, almost as confusing as Nimit's insistence that the distance between their two homes was only the tiniest fraction of the circumference of the world.

"Will we be able to see them?" The technologist glanced down the long cabin, careful to avoid eye contact with Zawadi.

"Not well."

Nimit wiped his right hand across the wall. A view of the triangular wedge of their craft appeared in the wake of his touch. Beneath it, a patchwork of emerald shot through with ochre and indigo flowed toward an endless horizon.

"We're very high up. The air here is incredibly thin, but even at this altitude..." Nimit shrugged, twisting his long curly hair.

The image rushed closer to the surface. Blurred outlines resolved into fantastic cathedral shapes, but the air around them boiled as if something unseen divided their craft from the strange landscape.

"This is as close as we can get. The people who built these are elusive and unappreciative of our advances, but we've seen signs of their power." Nimit circled the man, positioning himself beside Zawadi. "Whole cities floating on air, craft moving instantly many thousands of miles. They make us look like children."

"As *we* are to you," she said.

"Not children, partners." Nimit brushed his hand across her forehead, a gesture of affection among his people. His fingertips burned against her skin, and she lowered her gaze.

"I believe you."

"Forgive me for running away." Nimit dropped onto a couch beside Zawadi. He'd flitted from group to group for nearly an hour, explaining the aircraft's functions and softening fears, while Zawadi sat and fretted about the future. The further they traveled from her home, the less sure she became.

"I've been waiting to speak with you." She shouldn't ask, but she'd been told she'd have the rights of an equal under his laws. "About the agreement."

She glanced at her knees, her face flush. Her dark, chocolate-colored skin glistened as if freshly oiled. His gaze followed hers, and she wondered why a eunuch would covet the flesh of a woman. She wished she knew more of his customs, so she could ask what would be required of her, but the betrothal had been hurried. Her father had all but sold her in exchange for assistance in his struggle with the people of the Endless Forest.

"I'd hoped you would look on this as an adventure, and not a death sentence." He winked, but his dark brown eyes didn't echo the humor of his words. "Not too many people get the chance to travel half a million miles from home."

Zawadi's stomach tumbled as nervousness ate at the lunch banquet she'd tried so hard to enjoy. Nimit's offer had opened possibilities. At home, and as the youngest daughter, she'd never be in control of her own destiny. Now, away from the crushing responsibilities of court, things might be different.

"You're right. It's a great honor, but..."

He smiled, studying her. "But you're frightened. I understand."

"They told me I had a choice." She blurted it out, terrified she was wrong, but unable to wait any longer. "By the Republic's laws, I don't have to consent to the marriage pact."

Nimit's expression softened. He leaned back in his chair, his usually playful features hidden by jeweled fingers. "If you're unhappy, it's your right to decline. But at least wait until we arrive."

She nodded. Her expression must have appeared cold, especially after her initial excitement at having been chosen, but it was all too new and puzzling.

"It's just..." She struggled to put her jumbled thoughts into words. She didn't want to insult him. His people were amazingly powerful, but she didn't want to be anyone's wife. Not now, not yet. "I don't..."

9

"You don't have to make a decision right away. We have days to get to know each other before reaching the Republic."

She searched the length of the aircraft's cabin. Its contours flowed like glass, liquid blue lines sweeping in graceful arcs from floor to ceiling, bulging only to accommodate the twelve sumptuous couches spaced in four roughly circular groups.

"Why did you even choose me?" She said it quickly, breathlessly. She wanted to know why he'd chosen a girl when he could've had a woman. Why had Nimit taken the gift of a wife when he must have known she'd be a spy?

"You seemed softer than the others. I thought you might be easier to teach." He crossed his legs in a very feminine gesture.

Zawadi wondered if he meant sexually. Nimit was a difficult man to read. For the most part he was playful and at ease, a man comfortable with himself, but there were times when he seemed every bit the ambassador caught in a marriage arranged for the sake of alliance. He was very different from the men at her father's court. She liked him, and it made her uncomfortable with the part she'd been expected to play.

"Just give it time," he said. "We have plenty—"

The floor shrieked. Walls rippled and shattered. Nimit slammed into the ceiling as the cabin lurched. The lights went out. A woman screamed, and the smell of burning rubber filled the air.

Zawadi fell to her knees, choking.

The floor dropped again, tossing her against a table. She tasted blood. Her lower lip stung, and sharp tics of pain jabbed her right eye. She couldn't breathe. Her heart pounded, her body trembling with every heave of her lungs. She didn't want to die, not so far from home.

A bluish glow slithered across the floor. Nimit's face hovered above it. Shadows sputtered, and the lights returned.

"Are you okay?" A dribble of blood leaked from his nose. He crawled to Zawadi, and together they fell onto one of the soft couches.

"What happened?" Zawadi fought to control her breathing. Her experience with flying had been localized, confined to the balloons of her father's kingdom. She had no frame of reference for this supersonic ship, no way of knowing how seriously they were damaged, and that made it all the more frightening.

A shrill hiss ripped through the cabin. The craft lurched, tumbling. Zawadi clung to the divan. Her fingers dug into the plush fabric, straining as everything spun around her.

Nimit slid across the floor. His fingers left a trail of pale azure light as he clutched for purchase. Frosted partitions fell in slices across the cabin, cutting them off from the others. The ship shuddered, and then stilled.

Zawadi wanted to throw up. She gasped for air, sobbing as she fought to control the feeling they were falling to their deaths. Smudged shapes moved against the glass, and a child cried. Others were alive.

"I'm sorry." Nimit lay in a heap against the partition, struggling in feeble spurts to pull himself up. His lips were smeared with blood.

"Don't talk." She pulled him onto her lap, cradling his head. His eyes wouldn't focus on her. "You'll be fine."

He dragged his arm across the floor, creating one of his blue-tinged windows, and leaving a smear of blood. He poked the image of their craft, tilting it with a swipe of his finger. "We're falling." He wheezed, his words coming in the peaks of heaving breaths. "There are safeguards. Helium filled baffles to slow our descent, but... nowhere to land."

"Save your breath." She held him with her trembling hands, trying not to cry.

Zawadi had wanted so much to get away, leave the confines of her home and choose her own destiny, but fate had a way of playing tricks. Home had been boring, but at least it'd been safe. She couldn't think of anything she wanted more than to be back there right now.

Sharp banging startled her. It came from beyond the glass wall, and she remembered they weren't alone. Others were going to die.

"I've called for help." Nimit twisted the image, doing something with his fingers that made the scene look like a painting. A blue smudge peeked from the forward edge. A tiny pink dot glowed near a wide swath of green on the opposite side, and a gold triangle hovered in the center. "But we're many thousands of miles from the Republic."

"Is that us?" She pointed to the triangle.

"The Republic on this side. Your home over here." He touched the blue and then pink patches. "Half a million miles between them, and we're nowhere near either."

Zawadi sagged, the enormity of their situation draining the life from her. "What do we do now?"

"We wait..." Nimit's voice faded. He coughed, blood staining his lips.

"Can *they* help?" Zawadi had been studying the landscape. Faint outlines of a massive city were visible just outside the aircraft's projected flight zone. She wasn't familiar with the world beyond her own kingdom, but the people below looked more than advanced enough to save a falling aircraft.

He shook his head. "No. I'd spoken about them earlier, one of the hyper-advanced civilizations. They'll do nothing unless provoked, and we would not want to provoke them."

"Would they kill us?"

"I don't think so." He took a deep shuddering breath, gasping as he struggled to change position. "We've never seen violence, just a desire to be left alone and the power to enforce it."

He stroked the graphic of their craft with two fingers, plucking it like a stringed instrument. "I signaled an emergency, but there's no response. I don't even know if they're listening."

Zawadi studied his pale, blotchy features. Nimit closed his eyes. His breathing shallowed, a raspy wheeze from deep inside. He wouldn't last much longer.

The toddler started crying again. Zawadi wondered what had become of the child's parents. The man in the orange suit had handled her with such firm authority. The little girl wouldn't be crying if...

She tried not to think about it, but what had Nimit said about the society below them? They viewed less advanced peoples as children. Would they treat the aircraft as the man in the orange suit had treated his daughter? Would they simply put them where they belong?

She jammed her fingers into the screen. The gold triangle felt icy, a frigid spot on the warm floor, and it stung as she twisted it. The cabin swayed in time with her gestures.

She didn't care. It was time to provoke someone.

"I'm sorry I brought you on board." Nimit struggled with the words, his voice slurring and pained. "I'm sorry I put your life in jeopardy."

She didn't know how to reply. She shouldn't have accepted his offer, but she'd been so desperate—too desperate—and her options had been limited. There'd been something about Nimit that had intrigued her. He was exotic, different. It'd been enough to take the chance, and she'd have to live or die by that choice.

"Forgive me for asking, but I still don't know what a eunuch would want with me."

He chuckled, the last thing Zawadi had expected. His dark glossy eyes widened. "Who told you I was a eunuch?"

"I'm so sorry. I'd assumed..." She covered her mouth, her face warming as she glanced away. "From our conversations, I just thought..."

He leaned in. She tensed. He looked as if he'd kiss her, his eyes bright as if he were just about to share a joke. "I haven't made up my mind yet."

He fell against the partition, the smile lingering on his lips.

"Stay with me. I don't want to be alone." She shook him, suddenly terrified. She didn't want to die alone. "Keep talking. Don't go, not yet. I want to know, was it *me* you were unsure of?"

His eyes fluttered. He gripped her hands, his fingers hot, and his skin soft and moist. "Not you, *me*. I haven't chosen a gender."

"You haven't... what?"

"No gender. I'm sexless, but I *will* choose... eventually."

She stared, not knowing what to say or how to react. It couldn't be possible to be... nothing. A person had to be one thing or the other, didn't they? She'd made assumptions based on the way he walked, the way he spoke and acted, but she could never have guessed she'd be wrong no matter which she chose.

"My people believe we have the right to be whatever we want, even if we don't know what we want, like me." His voice lost its playful edge, becoming serious. "It's not an easy decision."

Zawadi still couldn't comprehend how a person could be *without* gender. There were certain physical limitations, weren't there?

"You're not male?"

"No."

"But you might become female?" Zawadi's curiosity overwhelmed her manners.

"Would that bother you?"

"No, my people have no such taboo. I'm just... fascinated and confused at the same time."

She glanced at the wreckage around her; broken plastic, smashed wood and glass, and smears of blood clinging to the glass divider. Did it really matter? How long would it be before they were dead anyway?

"If it's about the marriage contract, you never had to accept. I wouldn't have bound you that way."

"How will I know without being sure which you'll become?"

"My people have a saying." Nimit smiled, a warm grin on a friendly face. She could have grown to love that face in time. "Chose the singer, not the song."

A sheering shriek rattled the cabin. The floor shifted. Zawadi screamed, clutching Nimit as they slid into the wall. The aircraft tilted. Nimit landed on top of her, his ragged breath hot on her cheek.

"The baffles are giving out." He struggled to reach the screen. "We're falling faster now."

The ground was much closer. She could make out features through the growing clouds. Hazy white outlines filled her view. They were so close, and yet so much further from safety. Zawadi thought about the promises Nimit had made, the wonders he'd have shown her. It would've been amazing. Then she thought about her home, her father's court and her overbearing sisters. It hadn't been the worst place in the world.

"Forgive me." Nimit squeezed her hand. His grip weakened as he lost consciousness.

Zawadi wrapped her arms around his chest, laying her head in the crook of his arm. The sky boiled. Individual buildings became visible, cloudy silhouettes fading in and out. Her heart fluttered. She tried to control her breathing, telling herself it would be quick.

The lightheaded rush of falling intensified. The cabin rattled, shaking harder. An inner calm enveloped her as they sliced through the atmosphere, and she wasn't afraid anymore.

"I have a secret." She whispered. Nimit's breathing softened, as if he could hear her. "I've already made my choice."

Gender didn't matter, location didn't matter. She hoped for a miracle, but if the people below didn't save them and they died right here, she wouldn't care. She'd chosen the singer, and not the song.

About The Author

D. A. D'Amico is a playful soul trapped in the body of a grumpy old man. In early years, this presented a problem, but the author's grown into the role quite nicely. He's had more than forty works published in the last few years in venues such as Daily Science Fiction, Crossed Genres, and Shock Totem... among others. He's also begun transcribing his memoirs onto the moon with a 25 petawatt pulse laser borrowed from his evil twin, but he's afraid the beautiful 12-point Old Century Gothic font he chose is lost among the bright dust of Tycho crater. He can be found at http://www.dadamico.com or on Facebook at authordadamico, or in the crevices between those pesky floorboards you've been meaning to fix—if you can find him.

Available
from Founders House and other Booksellers

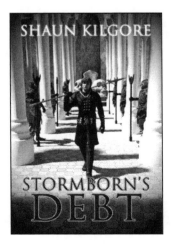

HIS BRILLIANT EYES

BY AARON EMMEL

He would escape tonight.

Jake tied the blue paisley scarf back over his face before he went out to the living room. His mother was already waiting. "Have a good sleep," she told him in her deep, calming voice as she pressed the pill into his palm. She smiled her gentle smile, but as always she avoided looking into his eyes.

"Thank you." His breath was moist and warm against the cloth that hung in front of his mouth. He started to turn.

"Jacob," she said. "Swallow it here, will you?" Her fingers tapped her thighs. "I want to make sure you don't have another bad dream."

He nodded and pushed the pill up beneath the scarf. He slid it between his teeth and swallowed. Even though his face was covered he didn't try to trick her. She would know. Somehow, she always did.

But she didn't know yet about the key. Did she? He quickly scanned her face. There was nothing in her expression to suggest she thought anything

was wrong. But it was only a matter of time.

Stay calm. Don't give anything away.

"You know that we just want to protect you," she said.

Why had she said that? Was it something about his body language? "Yes," he said.

"Good night, Jacob."

"Good night." He retreated to his room and shut the door firmly behind him, wishing it had a lock.

Jake picked up the battered metal Superman trash can in the corner and held it between his knees as he sat down on the bed. He was eighteen, but he was still surrounded by the trappings of childhood.

He had used the family laptop to look up ways to induce vomiting. Ever since his dad had found his cached searches about committing suicide he had been careful to delete his browser history. That incident was one of the reasons for the pills.

Eighteen years trapped in this trailer and its yard. Eleven years of homeschool. They had taken vacations, but always to remote places where the chance of spending much time with other people was slim. That was justification enough to want to end things. Erasing his childhood memories wasn't going to solve anything.

Although maybe it had, because tonight he didn't intend to die. He was going to escape.

He thrust two fingers down his throat and heaved. His vomit was hot and acidic. He was surprised at how exhausted he was afterwards. He spent a few minutes leaning forward with his hands on his knees as his stomach convulsed.

He wiped his lips and let the trashcan fall to the floor. He didn't want to leave the mess for his parents to clean up. But he had no choice. After that he waited, his muscles rigid, afraid to move in case he did something to trigger his parents' attention, until he heard them get ready for bed and turn off the TV and close the door to their room. Silence settled over the house. It was only then that Jake reached beneath the mattress he was sitting on and pulled out the key.

His window was alarmed. For his safety, his parents had always told him. That made the front door the only way out.

He tugged on his rubber-soled sneakers, slipped into his jacket and picked up his Swiss Army knife and a pair of rubber gloves he had purchased on Amazon. He adjusted his cotton scarf and made sure it was firmly in place. Then he opened the door and left his bedroom for the last time. He knew every minute detail of that space, and it never even occurred to him to pause or look back.

Every footstep he took, every breath he exhaled, seemed unbearably loud. He strained his ears listening for movement from his parents' bedroom. But he heard nothing other than his own movements as he traversed the short hallway, the carpeted living room, the kitchen with its linoleum flooring. Then, finally, he was at the trailer's front door. He typed the alarm code into the keypad. The light switched from red to green. That's when he heard movement from his parents' room behind him.

He reached into his jeans pocket and fished out the key.

His parents' door opened. "Jacob?" his mom asked. "Is everything all right?"

He jammed the key into the lock— "the lock is there to protect you"—and twisted.

"Jacob!" his mom shouted, running toward him. "What are you doing?"

Jake pulled open the door and flung himself down the steps.

"Frank!" his mom shouted behind him. "Frank, wake up! Jacob's getting out!"

Instinct pulled him away from the house, toward the gated fence, but instead Jake veered to the left, around the side of the trailer to the junction box. He unlatched the metal door, pulled it open and flipped the switch to de-electrify the fence. Inside the trailer, a superfluous alarm went off.

He heard his mom's footsteps gaining as he left the box and ran for the fence. Behind her the trailer's front door crashed open again as his dad emerged. Jake tugged on his gloves, slowing and stumbling as he did so. Then he was at the fence. In his mind he was already scrambling up over it. But instead he skidded to a halt. Looking out at the grassy field beyond the fence, the line of shadowy pines forty yards out, the two-lane strip of pockmarked asphalt that skirted the woods and led to the rest of the world, he felt vertigo so suddenly and strongly that his knees started to buckle and he almost fell.

It wasn't safe out there. That was the reason for the pill, and the locks, and the electricity. His parents protected him. They kept him safe from the people out there who would use him, who would cause him harm.

He shook his head and took a step backward.

"Jacob," his mom pleaded breathlessly as she reached him. "We can't take care of you out there."

He felt the warmth and weight of her body lean into his, her fingers brushing his arm as her hand started to close around his wrist.

He launched himself up, grabbed onto the high-tensile wires, and climbed.

"Jacob!" his mom called up from below. "It's not safe out there!"

Jake hauled himself to the top of the fence and perched there for a moment, looking out, afraid to drop to the ground. Afraid of the outside.

The electricity surged on.

It felt like he had plunged his hands into a pile of ants. He felt the vibrating sting beneath his rubber gloves and on the back of his neck.

"Frank!" his mom shrieked. "Frank, turn it off! He's on the fence! Frank!"

Jake fell through the air and hit the ground. The breath from his lungs burst out of his mouth. He tried to roll as he hit, but the impact slammed through his muscles to vibrate his bones. His vision went black and he blinked until he could see hazy shapes again. His mom was screaming. He raised his head to look up at her, and realized with some surprise that there was a web of wires between them. He was on the other side of the fence.

He crawled.

He dragged himself through the dirt and grass. He passed out, once, against the trunk of a half-dead juniper. When he came to he saw that he was in the woods. Dark trunks rose in every direction, sentinels with splayed limbs and needle-sharp claws. He pulled himself up and patted himself. His entire body was sore, but fortunately nothing seemed broken. He started walking.

It was slow going, picking his way over roots and around rocks. A breeze came up and he zipped up his jacket.

They just wanted to protect him. They wanted what was best for him.

But he would rather face whatever risks were out here than spend the rest of his life on a two-and-a-half acre prison.

The moon was on its descent into the western sky by the time he willed himself to slide down into the dry brush that bordered the highway. He could make quicker time there than in the hills, but occasionally, even out here in the middle of nowhere and at this hour, there were cars and long-haul trucks. Every time he saw headlights he dropped down and pressed himself into the dirt.

Don't talk to strangers. Don't look at them. They're dangerous.

He slept for a few hours against a bed of boulders halfway up a hillside hidden from the road. He woke shivering as darkness leaked out of the east-ern sky and the outline of distant mesas emerged with the dawn. His joints were stiff and cold. He hiked back down to the highway.

A short time later he came to an intersection where the old highway he was following met up with the interstate. There was a cluster of buildings surrounding the crossroads, blocky buildings etched dark against a brittle morning sky.

The closest building was a convenience store. "ALLSUP'S," the sign read, red letters on a white background. From behind a screen of juniper and sage he watched a tall, thin man emerge from the glass doors with a giant plastic soda cup and a paper-wrapped burrito. Jake's stomach knotted itself in hunger.

Don't talk to strangers.

He turned away from the store. Keep walking, he told himself.

By late morning he had left the brush and was trudging through the dirt on the side of the road, no longer bothering even to turn his head when cars roared past. Dust swirled up with every footstep. His shirt clung to his back with sweat. The sun blazed white in a limitless sky. The next time he saw a convenience store, a 7-Eleven behind two rows of gas pumps, he didn't hesitate. Hunger tugged him across the parking lot and past the door.

He wandered the aisles twice before he picked anything up, overwhelmed by his hunger and the choices. Finally he started filling his hands: Flamin' Hot Cheetos, a 40 ounce Big Gulp, Twix. His hands full, he started hugging his haul in his arms: beef jerky, Nacho Cheese Doritos. The packages were starting to slip through his fingers and he was afraid that if he squeezed the drink much more the lid would pop off, so he deposited everything on the front counter.

The fortyish clerk had been watching him the entire time. Now he said, "There are cops on their way."

"Why?"

"Is this a holdup?"

"No."

"Then maybe you take off the mask."

"It's not a mask. It's a scarf."

"I don't have to serve you." He pointed at one of the many signs on the wall behind him, between a warning about bad checks and a notice that alcohol would not be sold to minors. This one read, *We reserve the right to refuse service to anyone*.

"It's not a holdup."

"Then why you have the mask?"

"I have to wear it. It's for my protection."

A woman had wandered into the store behind him. "Some people have conditions," she told the clerk. "Or surgery or something like that. Give him a break."

The clerk glared at her. "You've been robbed? You've been held up? What do you do if he's a robber, huh? You going to defend me?"

"Listen," Jake said, "I just want to get this stuff. Then I'll be out of here. No problems. I promise."

"Fine." The clerk shrugged and rang up his order and gave him a price.

Jake paused. "Okay. Can I put it on my tab?"

"What tab? What do you mean, tab?"

"Like on TV. When people go to restaurants. Sometimes they have a tab. I'd like to use that."

"No tab. What are you talking about? You don't have money?"

"No." He had thought about stealing some from his parents, but that had seemed like too extreme a bridge to cross. At home his parents had let him use their credit card for his infrequent online purchases.

"You have a credit card?"

"No."

The clerk glared at him and stabbed buttons on his cash register. "Get out now or I'm calling the cops."

"You said you'd already—"

"I mean it."

Jake started to pick up the merchandise to return it to its shelves.

"Get out of here."

Jake looked at him. For the first time their gazes locked. The clerk's eyes widened. His expression softened

19

and he froze, as if mesmerized. Jake waited a moment. Then he left the items on the counter and stepped back out into the heat.

He imagined turning around and finding his way back home. He imagined his parents running out to open the gate for him. He saw them pulling him into their arms. *I'm so sorry I left,* he heard himself say. *I swear I'll swallow the pills. I'll never try to escape again.*

His muscles ached from his fall and his nap on the ground, and his mouth was so dry it hurt to swallow. Soon all of his energy, all of his thoughts, went into putting one foot in front of the other. He felt his stomach roil and willed his legs to keep moving.

The sun burned in the middle of the sky. Cars flew past in both directions, buffeting him with the wind of their passage.

It was early afternoon when he reached the town. It was a settlement of houses and trailers that hugged the highway close to where it met a low, sluggish creek. First he passed small farms and pastureland where cows grazed listlessly on sparse grass, and then houses with big yards set back from the road. In the middle of the town were a Presbyterian church, a Catholic church, a post office, a gas station and a general store. And after that a diner, with a handful of vehicles parked outside. Jake entered.

The restaurant's air conditioning was running on high and it smelled like chili and grease. His mouth watered. The lunch crowd, if there had been a crowd, was gone now, and two guys with flannel shirts and stubble beards walked out just as he came in. The only other customers were a family of three at one of the tables and a man and a woman in business dress talking across an iPad and a stack of papers in a booth. The family was a couple in their thirties with a daughter of about seven. The girl was energetic and talkative. Her parents had the slow-moving, slack-faced appearance of the chronically sleep-deprived.

"If you want to eat here you'll have to take that off." It was the server, a man in his early twenties with a button-up shirt and black pants.

"Do you have tabs here?"

"What do you mean, 'tabs'?"

"Like, if you want to pay over time—"

"You can't pay?"

"I can, but over time, if—"

"I'm going to have to ask you to leave." The server said this with an unhurried firmness that suggested he had rehearsed the line in his mind.

Jake placed his palms on the table. He sorted through a list of possible responses. But none of them would get him food or rest, and he was too tired to think about anything else. He stood up.

The server nodded and headed for the kitchen.

Instead of walking to the exit Jake made his way to the bathroom. There was only one room, unisex. He reached the door just after the seven-year-old girl did. She stared at him inquisitively. "Why are you wearing a mask?" she asked.

"It's a scarf."

She frowned. "Okay, but why?"

"It's to protect me."

"From what?"

"Strangers."

She frowned again, but continued on into the bathroom. He waited outside. A few minutes later she came out wiping her hands on her pants and he entered, pulling the door shut after him.

He untied his scarf, peeled off his shirt and splashed water over his face. Then he used paper towels to scrub his torso and under his arms. He cupped his hands and slurped up the water from the faucet, again and again and again.

The door opened. The mother saw him and froze in the process of entering. "Oh my God! I'm so sorry."

"It's all right," he said, grabbing his shirt.

She didn't move. She was still staring at him. But not his awkward, protective pose, or his bare chest. His face.

She was mesmerized, like the 7-Eleven clerk had been, but as she walked slowly into the tiny bathroom, as she pushed the door shut behind her, as her fingers twisted home the lock he had neglected, as she stepped up against him so that their bodies—hers clothed, his half-naked—were touching, he saw something else. Hunger. She tugged the shirt out of his hands and kissed him.

He brushed his fingers once against her straw-blond hair and drew them away. Then he brought them back, feeling each soft lock slip through his fingers as her craving consumed him, as her hunger became his.

He didn't know how much time had passed, but her pants were on the floor when he heard her husband outside in the hall. "Deb? Are you in there?"

She kissed Jake harder to prevent him from making a noise.

"Deb?"

She pushed him against the sink.

Five minutes later she stepped back, adjusted her bra, pulled down her shirt, zipped up her Lees. She gazed at him again. "You're so beautiful," she whispered. She unlocked the door and walked out. The door clicked shut behind her.

Jake sat down on the toilet seat and felt sick. He saw the girl's face. He heard the husband's voice. What had just happened? What had he done? He

21

washed his hands again, and then his face, but he didn't feel any cleaner. When he walked out Deb's husband was waiting for him.

The punch snapped Jake's head to the side and sent him reeling back against the bathroom door. The crack of the man's knuckles on his jaw reverberated through his skull. Jake swallowed salty blood. He lunged and swung for the stomach as another blow glanced off his ribs. When Jake's fist connected the man let out a gasp and his upper body dropped like a marionette's, but as his torso folded he threw his arms around Jake's back.

The two men grappled, grunting as their feet scraped the floor and Jake's shoulders banged the wall. The husband found Jake's neck and squeezed. Jake grabbed his wrists as the man's fingers tightened. He smelled the man's sweat and heard his ragged breath against his ear. The world swam. *I shouldn't have run*, he thought to his parents. The husband looked into his eyes.

It took a moment for Jake to realize the man had stopped moving. Slowly, not taking his eyes off of Jake's face, the husband released his grip and backed away until he had left Jake alone in the hall.

After a few minutes Jake walked back out to the dining room. The family was leaving the restaurant, their food mostly uneaten. Deb wore a stunned, despairing expression. She and her husband both avoided looking at him. The chair Jake had sat in before was still pulled out and he sank down into it.

His lips and jaw throbbed. He touched his mouth and his fingers came back bloody. He had left his scarf in the bathroom. He started to rise to go back for it, but he was blocked by the server.

"I'm just leaving," Jake said.

The server dropped a plate onto the table. An eight ounce sirloin steak, a baked potato and green beans. Then he set down a napkin, a fork and a steak knife beside it.

"I'm sorry I was so rude earlier," the server told him. He was looking at Jake's face with something like awe. Jake could feel the eagerness to please radiating from him. "I don't know why I was so rude."

"I can't pay for this," Jake said.

"It's on the house. Don't worry about it." The server backed away. "I'm sorry." Jake sliced off a chunk of the meat. Seared on the outside, just slightly pink in the middle. He put it in his mouth and chewed. Maybe it was just his imagination, but his body felt stronger, his mind more alert, the moment he swallowed. He cut off another piece.

Meanwhile the couple in the booth had raised their voices. One of them, the woman, walked over to the server and confronted him near the service window. After a moment the cook came out, wiping his hands on his apron. The woman turned to the cook, gesticulating angrily, and he turned to shout something at the server.

Jake ignored them and had another bite of steak. And then another.

The conversation near the kitchen was growing more heated. Jake glanced back at the booth the woman had come from. The man was still there, his plate of food uneaten and growing cold. It was the only plate on the table.

The server gave me the woman's food, Jake realized.

He swallowed down the meat he was chewing and slowly pushed his plate away. This is what it will be like wherever I go, he thought. I'll destroy everything I come in contact with.

Now that he had this trigger, now that he knew what to look for, the memories his parents had tried to get him to suppress came flickering back. The kids in the schoolyard who had lined up for his approval. The teachers who made him king of their classrooms. The resentment. The fights.

Maybe he could go back home.

No. That life had only been possible because he hadn't been aware of the impact he was having. Even when he had remembered his abbreviated school experience he hadn't truly understood it until now. Now he appreci-

ated the fear his parents had of him. For him, yes, but also of him.

Or maybe he had known. Maybe he had guessed that his parents hadn't put up a high-voltage fence just to keep out elk and the occasional coyote. Maybe he had lied to himself. Maybe he had needed the pills his mother gave him to make himself forget. But he was eighteen. How much longer could he live as an adult with the two people who most loved him but were most terrified of him?

He picked up the steak knife.

A slice across the face, he thought. Start at the corner of the eye. He pressed the rounded tip against his skin, felt the serrated edge dimple his cheek. Cut down to the chin. If he did it quickly enough then he might be able to slash both sides before the pain incapacitated him. Would that end it? Would that erase whatever it was people saw when they looked at him, let them see him as just another man?

He moved the knife to his left wrist. A single long, deep, lengthwise stroke. That was the only way he could be certain of ending it.

Someone was standing above him. It was the woman, come to yell about the steak. He met her eyes.

Her face melted. He saw the craving there, felt it. Felt it ignite the need within himself, felt that spark flare more quickly now, felt it burn stronger as he became accustomed to it.

"My name is Rebecca," she said, thrusting out her hand. "Rebecca Gaines. I'm a political consultant. I don't mean to interrupt, but have you ever considered running for office?"

Jake let the knife slip out of his fingers and clatter on the table. He gave her a small smile and shook her hand.

About The Author

Aaron Emmel's fiction has appeared in numerous magazines and anthologies. Find him online at: www.aaronemmel.com.

PULLING SECRETS FROM STONES

BY BETH GODER

In the lakebed by the mountains slept stones full of secrets. Waiting memories. Dissipating memories. Rachel could feel the hum of them, their longing for closeness, pressing against her as the sun pressed down.

She slid down to the lakebed. Dust rose around her, obscuring her truck by the side of the road. The air stagnated, heavy and dry, baking itself into the earth.

Her memories were dying—the secret ones, the memories that let her touch the sky, the memories of how to cast a branch to find missing things, or summon a flower in her hand. All of her most important memories. Gone.

She pulled a geological survey map from her pack, jostling her water bottle and a squished peanut butter sandwich. Unfolded, the map stretched farther than her arms. Red marks showed where she had searched. Not much of the map was marked—perhaps half an inch.

Rachel hiked until she reached the edge of her last red mark.

She turned over a stone—memory shaped—then cupped it in her hands. Ordinary. The next stone was the same, and the next. The lakebed stretched for miles, with huge cracks like fractals in the dust. Endless.

Stones, stones, stones. None of them memories.

Wind brushed past, and for a moment, Rachel feared that the woman in the mountains had found her. This close to the mountains, the woman could feel the land as if it were her body—the sweep of wind along mountain backs, the plants that thrust themselves through soil, the intrusion of sun into shaded spaces. The woman in the mountains had described this connection to Rachel, back when she had described everything to Rachel. Before the anger. Before the woman had discovered Rachel putting memories into stones. Before the rift that separated them as no mountain could ever do.

When Rachel looked up, only the sun was above her. Her relief was empty. Dry. As much as she feared the woman in the mountains, she wished to see her again.

And Rachel did fear her. The woman was like a crash of rain, an avalanche, soaking everything in her path. Unaware. But Rachel had come to love her wild kindness, her fierceness. The woman would mix the colors of the sunset beautiful and bright. She would send goats to look after the elderly, those who had no children. With a splash of soil and a whisper, she could cure sickness in trees, but never death.

The memory of the woman hung above Rachel like a dark sky, full and treacherous. Waiting.

Waiting as stones waited. Rachel grabbed another stone, rough and rounded. Ordinary.

She pulled the sandwich from her bag, wishing she had packed a more substantial lunch. Somewhere in the lakebed, locked in a stone, sat the secret of spontaneous berry pie. She remembered holding out her hands in the garden, a steaming boysenberry pie appearing among the flowers. But she couldn't remember how she'd done it, only that once she'd known the secret of it, when the lake was full, when water ran over the stones.

A crow circled overhead, dove, and landed on a boulder. "You'll never get anywhere that way," it said.

"No one asked your advice."

Of course, the only memory she'd found was the one that let her talk to birds. That memory stone was sitting in a bowl of water back at her apartment, submerged so that it would work.

"The way you are searching," said the crow, "so inefficient. Why did you store your secrets in pebbles?"

"I stored them in the lake." It was a good place for such memories. When the secret memories rubbed up against the regular ones—how to send a fax at the xerox store where she worked, the amount of coffee to put in the machine, the name of the guy who ran the junkyard—the magic became duller. She couldn't hold everything in her head.

And the other memories—the secret ones—they would change her if she let them get too close.

The crow shifted from foot to foot. One of its toes was missing. "Call the memories back to you. Call them from the stones. Secrets once yours will find you."

Rachel shook her head. There was safety in distance. Such a memory would twist through the pathways of her mind, changing what it found there. She could not afford such closeness. She wasn't like the woman in the mountains.

"Fill the lake with water. Summon the rain," said the crow, as if such a thing were simple.

"We all want the drought to end. I would have done it already if I could."

"You insist on being difficult." The crow picked up a stone in its beak, then tossed it away. "Talk to the woman in the mountains. She'll know where the rain went."

"She won't want to see me." Rachel grabbed another stone. Ordinary.

"Do not presume to know what the woman in the mountains wants," said the crow. "If you want your memories back, follow me."

The crow flew into the sky. It was headed in the direction of Rachel's truck.

When Rachel got back to her truck, the crow was sitting on the hood. It flapped its wings impatiently.

She patted the Toyota Stout, ignoring the crow. The Stout always made her feel better. Safer. Each part was known to her—valves and pushrods, radiator, gauges—all the parts that pushed against each other, all the parts she'd built into the engine. Solid. Logical.

She leaned into the truck's sturdy frame.

When she'd found the Stout in the junkyard, Rachel had been taking apart the engine of a Mazda Bongo van, just to see if she could put it back together. Across from the Mazda sat the Stout,

just like the one her dad used to drive. The outside was rusted in spots, but it had a strong engine—salvageable. She'd spent her weekends working on it, until it ran right.

The crow hopped to the car door and pecked. "The trip will be easier while the sun is still out."

"She won't help me."

The crow pecked again at the door. "I'll show you the way."

She looked to the sky, hoping for rain. In the drought, she'd lost the best part of herself. Rachel had forgotten how to make origami cranes that dispelled heartbreak as they flew over the town. She'd forgotten the location of the singing snakes, and the name for the nettles that could mend anything—a sweater, a bag, a bone.

Rachel climbed into the car and opened the door for the crow.

The mountain road was twisty, unkept, full of potholes. Her truck complained, shaking when it went over rough patches. She could picture the engaged engine—every moving part—almost as if the truck were an extension of her body, almost as if its murmur were her breath.

The crow perched on the passenger's seat, uncomfortable. It opened its wings, knocking into the stones she kept on the dashboard. Memory-shaped, but without memories. Not yet.

The truck made a bubbling noise. A sign that it was overheated. Not good.

She pulled over to the side of the road and grabbed her tools. The crow perched on her shoulder as she lifted the hood. Before her, the beautiful engine hummed. It was like a living thing, like a beating heart. An old heart. Every part, she'd touched with her hands. Every part knew her.

Steam rose from the truck. She'd have to let it cool off before she examined the engine.

"Bet you wish you had your memories now. The mending nettles would be useful, yes?" said the crow.

"I'd never use magic on the truck."

She didn't need magic to repair the Stout. Truck knowledge was a different kind of knowing. As a kid, she'd spent hours working on her dad's truck. He'd shown her how to salvage the best parts from the junkyard—shown her what was useable, even if it didn't look pretty, what was truly gone and rotted through. "Take stuff apart. Use the crowbar. Don't be afraid to get dirty," Dad had said.

Rachel sat on the side of the road. The crow perched on a stump.

"We're not so far, now," it said.

Rachel brushed dirt off her sleeve. "I don't expect I'll say much, when we find her."

"Don't you have anything left to say?"

Their relationship had been an imperfect thing, complicated by distance, cobbled together through kindness. Mostly, the woman's kindness.

She had shown Rachel how to find memories—the secret places to look. It was like searching in the junkyard. She had to look underneath to see what was really there, to see the potential of things.

Even after two years, the soreness from their last conversation wasn't gone. When the woman in the mountains had found the memory stones, she'd been furious. "This is not as I taught you," she'd said. She'd told Rachel to never come back.

The crow cocked its head, waiting.

"She has a different way," said Rachel. The woman in the mountains believed magic was like breath, running through all of life. Magic infused her, absorbed her. The memory stones were an abomination, she'd said. Lifeless. Distant.

"Different from your way," said the crow.

Rachel pointed to the truck. "The Stout, I know how it works—every piece, every part. If something's not right, I know where to look."

"And you think magic is different?"

"When the woman in the mountains taught me to pull flowers from my hands, when the roots embedded themselves, when the stems shot up from my skin—" Rachel couldn't describe how she'd felt—terrified, yes, but alive. The flowers had pulled at her skin, grown from her body, part of her. She hadn't felt pain, but a pressure. Sunlight on leaves. Wind on petals. "There's no way to understand how it works."

"You keep a dangerous distance," said the crow. "You want to hold a thing without letting it touch you."

"Necessary distance."

The crow fluttered its wings, then settled. "Not for the woman in the mountains. Do you remember what she taught you?"

"The stones remember."

"You kept nothing for yourself?" The crow shifted, flexing the foot with the missing toe. Rachel wondered if it could still feel the toe, the place where the toe had been.

She'd kept nothing of the magic. That was gone from her. But there were other memories—ordinary ones, true ones. "I remember flying," said Rachel. "The mountains were sharp against the sky, but I wasn't afraid. Not with her."

"You could fly again. Call the memory to you."

Rachel thought of secrets bottled in stones. She would not call to them. The crow should not ask.

The Stout was still steaming, but less now.

Rachel stood up. "The engine should be cool enough."

She leaned over the truck, hoping for an easy fix. Maybe a leaking hose. She revved the engine and watched the steam slide up. Not a hose—she could tell by following the flow of steam. She inspected the gasket. Not the problem. With trepidation, Rachel examined the radiator.

It was cracked.

She swore and gently closed the hood. They'd made it about three miles up the road, and the lake itself was two miles from town. The sun dipped lower in the sky.

She pulled a sleeping bag out of the truck and secured it to her pack. There was water, but no food. She hadn't expected to be out so long.

She could turn back, go into town. Come back the next day and repair the truck. Instead, she asked the crow, "How much farther?"

Rachel set out on foot, following the crow as it flew. She hiked for a mile over the winding road, until the crow flew over a side trail.

The trail twisted higher. At some points, it was barely a trail at all, obscured by rocks, covered by fallen trees. Not cleared in years—maybe not ever.

Although Rachel missed flying, it was good to hike.

The sunset lit the sky an intense purple. The crow flew down and perched on her shoulder, heavy. Talons pressed against her, all but the

29

missing one on the left foot. They had to be getting close.

"The woman in the mountains. Can you tell me—" Rachel took a breath. She needed to know if she was forgiven. If there was a chance of forgiveness.

The crow said, "Koww, koww."

Rachel turned to look at the crow.

The crow cawed, again and again. She couldn't tell what it was saying. She asked the crow to fly up, to lessen its grip on her shoulder, but it didn't. It couldn't understand her either.

She'd lost the ability to talk to birds.

Rachel thought of her memory stone in the bowl of water on her bookshelf. Something must have disturbed it. The cat. Her roommate. The memory couldn't work out of water.

The crow hopped off her shoulder, agitated. It danced around, pecking at the ground.

"Tell me where she is," said Rachel.

The crow grew, bulging in odd places. A wing became an arm. Toes grew from talons, one missing.

The crow stood, no longer a crow, but a woman.

The woman in the mountains.

Her hair had changed since Rachel had last seen her—it had grown longer, more wild. The hair wove around the woman, braiding itself, clothing her. She was smaller than Rachel remembered. And her eyes were harsher, dark blue and intense.

"Now we can speak properly," the woman said.

But Rachel couldn't speak. She wanted to ask forgiveness. She wanted to argue. Rachel had forgotten the wildness of the woman. Quick breath. Fierce smile. That smile sang of the world the woman had introduced—a world of possibilities and rawness, a world of secrets. The words Rachel did not say fell heavy like the air around her, charged and compressed.

At last, Rachel said, "Your toe."

"Gone," said the woman.

"An accident?"

"What is one toe, when I have the mountains, and the little streams that run through? The plants that weave over rocky soil. The sky. The sun that presses down."

"You didn't have to hide." Rachel thought of the crow perched on her shoulder, its talons pressing into her. Stolen closeness.

"I wanted to see if you were the same," said the woman.

"I haven't changed."

"No, you are so frightened of change. So frightened that you trap secrets in stones." The woman cast a stone into the air. It burst into dust. "A lake is not a place for secret memories. Now it is dry. Full of nothing, not even water."

Rachel thought of the landscape, dry where once it had been green. She imagined animals and people looking up to the sky, hoping for rain. "I never meant for that to happen."

"A drought is caused by many things. Only some blame falls on you."

"But you still blame me," said Rachel. "For everything."

"When I showed you how to find these secrets, I did not know you would hide them. I did not know you would be so afraid."

"I can't do what you ask of me." The memories had a wildness to them, elements Rachel couldn't control.

"You must choose," the woman said. "The stones cannot live in the lake. You must take the memories as your own, or not at all."

As she spoke, the woman opened her hands. Two flowers grew, poking up through her skin. The flower in her right hand became larger, blue. The flower in her left hand red and glossy.

Rachel looked at her own hands, where no flowers grew. She looked to the mountains and the wild sky. "I can't become like you."

"You would give up magic? And for what? A life you do not like? Your old truck that doesn't run?"

Rachel thought of the Stout, the engine she had labored on so long, the way all the pieces fit together to make something greater.

Rachel clasped the woman's hands, bringing the flowers together. The stems twined and grew, latching onto Rachel's skin, weaving her to the woman. The flowers merged and became as purple as the sky.

"To build an engine—it's not magic, but it's not an ordinary thing," said Rachel. The flowers twined around her arms. "It's somewhere in between."

"For you, it's not an ordinary thing."

"If I take the memories, they will change me," said Rachel.

"You'll be as I am."

"Not as you are. But not the same."

"Change is constant," said the woman. A new flower crept up to the sun. "You were changed the moment I found you in the junkyard, turning over engines to learn their secrets. You were changed by all the moments in your life before, and all the moments after. Do not be afraid of change. Bite it. Take the secrets between your teeth. Learn. Pull the memories to you."

Rachel stood with the woman, twined to her, the whisper of flower pulling at her arms. The flowers grew and bloomed, twisted and branched. The sun sunk lower in the sky, until purple became darkness. But still, Rachel did not pull the memories to herself.

"Will I see you again?" asked Rachel.

The flowers disappeared. The woman became a crow.

"Koww, koww," said the crow. "Koww, koww."

Rachel thought of her memories, trapped in stones, trapped where they should not be. She thought of flying through the evening sky, before the night had brought darkness, and the closeness of the wind. The weight of flowers on her hands. The crush of memory, a gentle wildness that pressed against her, but which she'd never held.

Tentatively, she pulled on the memory stone in her apartment, the secret language of birds.

The memory pried itself from the stone. Unbottled. Free. She could feel its pulse, like a new heart. It flew to her, over the dry lakebed, over the mountains. Home.

The memory submerged in her mind, awoken, alive.

The language twisted her mouth into odd shapes. Her thoughts reformed to speak in the language of birds—a mess of hunting, open sky, the night which leads to home or death.

With closeness came understanding, of a sort. But her heart was still a human heart. Undiminished. She felt as she had when flying. Unafraid, despite height and distance, despite the infinite sky.

"Will I see you again?" asked Rachel in the language of birds.

The crow who was not a crow flew up into the sky. The map in Rachel's pack leapt out and unfolded itself. A new symbol appeared, marking a spot in the mountains—two flowers twined together. A location. An offering. A way to find the woman again.

Rachel gathered up the map, then hiked down the trail until she found a sheltered space. The language of birds sang in her head, raw and wild, a part of her.

Miles down the road, the Stout waited for her, its radiator still cracked. Tomorrow, she would go to the junkyard and get what she needed to repair her truck.

Behind her, rainclouds loomed, blotting out the stars. A storm was coming.

About The Author

Beth Goder worked as an archivist before becoming a full-time writer and parent. Her fiction has appeared in *Escape Pod* and *Mothership Zeta*.

You can find her online at http://bethgoder.com or on Twitter at Beth_Goder.

"A TAUT, FAST-PACED THRILLER—NOT TO BE MISSED."
~ JOHN MICHAEL GREER

The industrialized world lies in ruins. Fossil fuels are gone. In isolated parts of the countryside after the Third World War, life goes on—however, the future looks more like the past.

In the 22nd century, a battle rages between the landowning Stakeholders who control Vermont's last biofuel refinery and the destitute farmers who have been forced to grow oilseed instead of food. When the aristocratic owner of the refinery is betrayed, his inventive son, Amariah Wales, allies with a mysterious rebel movement to destroy the Stakeholder's corrupt militia and restore the rule of law.

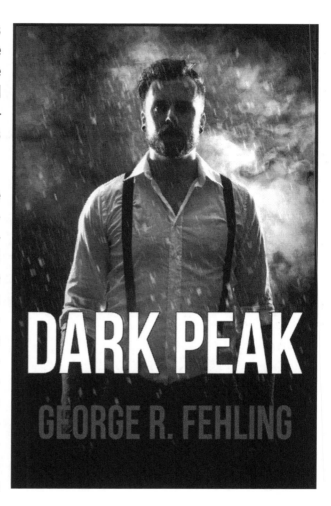

AVAILABLE FROM FOUNDERS HOUSE PUBLISHING AND OTHER BOOKSELLERS IN TRADE AND ELECTRONIC EDITIONS.

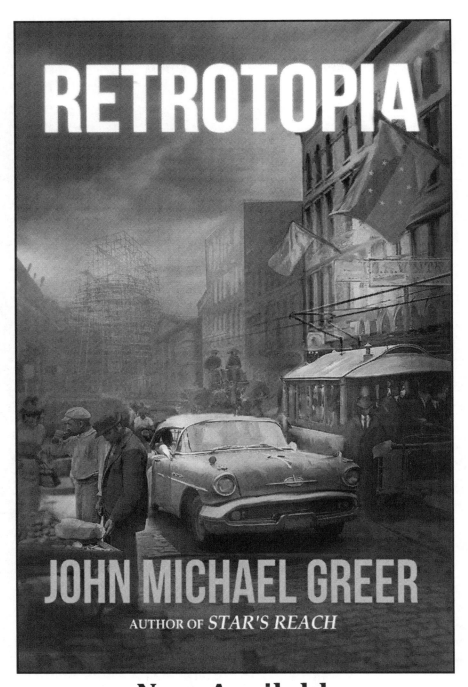

RETROTOPIA

JOHN MICHAEL GREER

AUTHOR OF *STAR'S REACH*

Now Available
from all your favorite booksellers
in trade paper and electronic editions

HUNTING THE BLACK DRAGON

BY ROBERT J. SANTA

Gadil grabbed Khalidah by the back of the collar, nearly choking her as he pulled her to the forest floor. Gadil knelt beside her, and as she rose to a crouch ready to punch him in the eye—sworn oath or no—she saw the mixed look of awe and fear in his face that she'd never before seen. He pointed through the border of the tree line at the rocky mountain peak. Khalidah followed his arm and saw a black smudge against the light brown and gray background. Gadil handed her the spyglass, and she looked again.

The dragon was beautiful. Jet black covered it, even the underbelly. Its body was far thinner than she had imagined; if it were a cat, she would have called it scrawny. But the breadth of its wings, outstretched to catch the afternoon sun, gave its sinewy length a majestic power, as if any more weight were an unnecessary extravagance. Khalidah couldn't see its head, for it was thrown back over its shoulders on a snake-like neck. She could feel the dragon's confidence in its command of the mountain, even from the valley floor.

Gadil clapped a hand on her shoulder, and she yelped. He scowled and aimed a come-with-me glare at her. She crawled away from the edge of the trees, only once looking over her shoulder to see if the dragon heard them.

"Master?" Khalidah called from the porch. "Someone comes."

She put away her broom and readied three castings, only two of which were defensive. It wouldn't be the first time raiders thought a few lonesome buildings would make for easy pickings. She raised the hood of her abaya and fixed the veil over her mouth and chin.

A lone rider moved between the trees. At first, it was the beautiful, black stallion that caught Khalidah's eye, for it was easily the finest horse she had

35

ever seen. Then she saw the man in the saddle, and the horse became as if a swaybacked mule.

He wore desert robes, but they could do nothing to conceal the power of his frame. His broad shoulders appeared to have pauldrons covering them, yet she knew no armor caused the robes to bulge as they did. The sleeves billowed up to his elbows and revealed forearms that looked chiseled from marble. Underneath the robes, his legs were covered in simple trousers and worn, goatskin halfboots - pauper's clothing.

And for all his ragged, barbarian appearance, his sword was the kind emperors lusted after their whole lives. Longer than any scimitar she had ever seen, with a handle that could fit even three of his massive hands, its blade lay hidden behind a scratched sheath. Wires that shone with silver purity wrapped the handle. On top of the pommel sat a gray and white gemstone so large it was as if a tern laid an egg there. Merely glimpsing the sword, Khalidah felt stirred to the point that she would give up Weaving forever merely to possess it.

The rider halted his mount twenty paces from the house without so much as pulling back on the reins or clucking his tongue. It was as if he willed the horse to stop, and it did.

"Your master is here?" the rider asked. It sounded not so much a question as a demand.

"I am, Gadil." He shuffled out from behind the door curtains, wiping his hands on a rag, which he dropped on the ground. Khalidah was convinced he had been aiming to drape it over the railing, which was a moot consideration since she would have bent to retrieve it even if he had flung it down like a scrap of meat for the dog. He was, after all, master. "When you said you would arrive between spring and summer, I did not realize it was supposed to mean a year later."

"The bastard king Fillipous decided to flex his young muscles."

"The year has made a difference in our arrangement, I'm afraid."

"You will no longer accompany me?"

"My lungs have been ravaged with the wasting disease. A journey of weeks is impossible for me now." As if the master had been bravely withholding the evidence, his body shook with wracking coughs.

"I see." Gadil sat upon his horse without either of them twitching a muscle, as if they were posing for a sculptor.

"My apprentice is almost finished with training," said the master. "Before the end of the year, I would make preparations for graduation. Perhaps my apprentice could assist you in your quest."

"Really, Samien?" Gadil lifted his foot out of the stirrup and laid his leg across the saddle. He rested his elbow on his knee and his chin in his hand. "And how do you propose an apprentice could be any help against a dragon?"

A dragon? Khalidah gave up all pretenses at eavesdropping and blatantly stared at the two men as they talked.

"Dragons can all but smell Essence," the master said. "I might be like a beacon. My apprentice's abilities, while great, may just be dimmed enough to avoid unwanted attention."

"Will they be so dim as to be useless? My request was for a powerful ally, Samien."

"And you will have it. Not even I, though, can be certain my castings would be strong enough. Dragons have a way of bending Essence. Even the young ones can do it."

"This is no hatchling; this is the Black Dragon."

"You would be surprised, Gadil, at my apprentice's abilities."

He sat upon the quiet horse and contemplated.

"Very well," Gadil finally said. "Send me your apprentice."

The master raised his hand, and Khalidah hurried over.

"Follow this man as you would me," he said to her. "Offer him all your skills. You will be acting in my stead."

Gadil's leg shot out from under him, and he bolted upright in the saddle.

"By the dog's...! You did not tell me your apprentice was a woman."

"How should it matter?"

"A woman, Samien?"

The master turned to Khalidah then searched the terrain. His gaze landed on a sandstone column one hundred paces west of the main house.

"If you please, Khalidah," he said.

She aimed the manipulation that had sat ready in her hand. The rock exploded like a sealed water jar thrown into a smith's furnace. Some smaller bits of debris rained down on them. To both the horse's and Gadil's credit, neither of them flinched. After all the dust had settled, Gadil spoke.

"She may come."

Khalidah spent the remainder of the morning gathering together a traveling bag. The master did nothing to help her and returned to his studies of sand beetles. She stood in the workroom doorway awaiting his farewell. He patiently drew the impaled bug, details magnified through a polished lens. A long while passed until she silently turned and went to the stables. She strapped a shelter and blankets to the saddle, filled the bags with her belongings and some items for her horse, then led it outside.

Gadil lay prostrate on a prayer rug. His beautiful horse grazed nearby. Khalidah found it odd that he had not removed the sword from his belt before praying then saw him rise up to his knees. He drew the blade and kissed it. Then he sheathed the sword so quickly it amazed Khalidah he had not severed a thumb.

He rolled up the mat and dropped it into a saddlebag. He gained his seat with a simple step into the stirrup, without a hint of bouncing. Khalidah, by contrast, led the horse to the porch so she could use its height to assist her. Gadil scowled at her. She was certain it would not be the last time.

Many hours passed in silence, punctuated only by the clopping of hooves on rocky paths. Just before nightfall, with the air cooling in a frightful rush, Gadil dismounted and drew a sling from his bags. He placed a rounded stone in the sling and swung it over his head. He released one thong into what seemed like open grassland. A soft impact sounded, followed by a high-pitched keening abruptly quieted. Gadil walked forward and bent down; his hand came up holding a dead hare. He put the sling in the saddlebag and handed the animal to Khalidah.

"Prepare this," he said, handing her the animal carcass. Then he searched the ground, occasionally bending down to pick up fallen wood.

Khalidah watched Gadil collect firewood. She took a knife and dressed the hare then impaled it on a long spitting iron retrieved from her saddlebags. Lastly, she sprinkled it generously with spices before laying it aside. As she removed the leathers from her horse, she saw Gadil wandering nearby. He loaded wood into a stack on one arm that must have weighed half what she did. He returned in a moment with the assortment of sticks and a small log dragging behind him.

"Make a fire," said Gadil, simply opening his arm and letting the wood drop into a pile beside Khalidah. Gadil turned, pulled the prayer mat from his bags, and walked a short distance away.

Khalidah ground her teeth as she stacked the wood. A simple gesture ignited it, and she leaned the iron against a long stick jammed into the earth. She contemplated the sizzling meat a moment then seasoned it again.

A long while later, Gadil joined her. His prayers had lasted until the sun had set behind the mountains, and following those he stripped and cleaned his horse. Khalidah spent her time finding potable water, some of it going into a pot of couscous finished with almonds.

"I am ready to eat," Gadil announced, and he held out his hand.

Khalidah spooned some couscous into a bowl, cut off one of the hare's legs and placed it on top, then handed the bowl to Gadil. He raised the meat and took a generous bite.

He immediately spat it onto the ground.

"Are you insane, woman? Did you use all the paprika?" he continued to spit as if a mouse had defecated inside his mouth.

"I find it quite tame," Khalidah replied. She lifted the other leg under her veil and ate heartily, without so much as a wince.

"This is disgraceful. Make new food."

"There is only one person who speaks to me the way you have, and I allow him to do it. I am here in my master's place. If you spoke to him the way you have me, he would blast your flesh from your bones. I expect the same respect." She took another bite of rabbit meat.

"Such an indignant woman!"

Khalidah flipped her hand. The fire roared, a column of flames that flew twice her height. Gadil fell away from it. He landed hard on his backside and stared at her openmouthed.

"My name is Khalidah. If you must insult my cooking or my person, at least do me the courtesy of using my name."

"Khalidah?" Gadil said it in a way that suggested he was testing its feel in his mouth.

She did nothing other than to tear the remainder of the meat from her rabbit's leg and chew slowly. Gadil tried another bite and made a face, though he maintained his quiet. Khalidah suppressed laughter as she watched him eat his meal.

Khalidah awoke to the sounds of a screaming child and a monster's hideous growling.

The fire had burned down to embers; only the softest, orange glow issued forth. She could see no further than a few paces beyond its faint light. A shuffling scraped the ground behind her, and she rolled over to stare into the jaws of a wolf.

It lay on its side, mouth agape, tongue lolling onto the sandy grass. It wriggled. Khalidah jumped to hands and knees, but the wolf remained lying down. It whimpered and vomited blood. She saw that it had been cut in two, its hips and lower legs nearby.

A second wolf lay headless. Gadil stood with blade drawn and dripping. A primitive syllable rumbled in his throat.

Another wolf leapt silently out of the firelight's periphery. Its teeth flashed a mere half-step from Gadil's flank. Khalidah saw a blur of motion,

39

and Gadil held the wolf by the throat. He let the momentum of its leap spin them both around as he whipped the wolf over his shoulder. He slammed it into the ground like laundry against a rock, and it was still.

Whimpers and soft, padded steps disappeared into the dark. Gadil held the naked blade as he gathered all three wolves' severed parts. He dragged them off until she could no longer hear his footsteps. His return was prefaced by not so much as a crunch of sole on gravel, and she tried not to show her surprise though she was certain he had seen it.

Gadil gathered a cloth from his bag and cleaned the sword of blood. Khalidah thought it faintly luminescent as it clung to the blade, but on the cloth it was just red.

Gadil lay the sword down on his mat and joined it.

"It is your turn for watch," he said. He inhaled and exhaled deeply once then was asleep.

Khalidah watched him until the sun rose. His sleep was as peaceful as if he lay under downy covers. His cheek didn't twitch at all, despite the blood drying on it.

"Why don't you carry a weapon?"

Gadil had stopped the horses at the peak of the first foothill. They could see the golden beginnings of the desert to the east, and the jagged, ugly mountains stretched out before them. The horses drank deeply from a pond while Khalidah filled jugs.

"I'm a Weaver," said Khalidah, and it was obvious to her that the answer was insufficient.

"Your talent cannot save you from every situation. A simple weapon can prove quite handy."

"With all due respect to your sword mastery, I am capable of defending myself."

"I say you are not."

Khalidah pushed the stopper into the jug and shook her head. Without warning, Gadil covered the ten paces between them in a few, powerful pounces. The sword sighed out of its sheath. It touched her ear like a lover's kiss.

"I could have taken your head," Gadil said matter-of-factly. "You didn't even rise out of a crouch."

"To defend myself from you?" Khalidah felt her face flush and hoped Gadil would think it from anger. "We are not enemies. In a place of true danger, I would be prepared."

"I see." Gadil turned and paced back to beyond where he had been standing. He returned his scimitar to his sheath and faced her. "I will kill you now. Prepare yourself."

Khalidah formed a casting with each hand: a shield and a paralysis.

With both arms raised, Gadil was suddenly before her. The sword slapped her head, the point on her neck. A bright flash blinded her for an instant.

"Tonight you will learn to fight with your hands," Gadil announced. He turned from her, the blade back in its scabbard. She didn't even see him sheathe it. She dismissed the shield and readied a blasting, then set it aside. She swore—albeit inside her head, and she wondered later how binding it was with no witnesses—not to do any harm to this infuriating swordsman. It made her feel marginally better, at least enough not to reduce him to ashes. That thought alone carried her through the rest of the day.

Yet hours later, as she splashed water on her face, her muscles screaming for mercy, she wondered whether it would have been simpler just to blast Gadil with a Weaving. They had made camp well before sundown, tended to the horses, built a fire and had a small meal of dried apricots and pistachios. Then he wandered off. Gadil returned a short while later with a straight birch limb three or four hands taller than Khalidah.

"Seems a bit long for a sword," she said.

"There is not enough time to teach you the ways of the sword," he replied, tossing the limb to her. She caught it and noted its considerable heft. "This is a spear. We will harden it in the fire tonight. Now hold it behind the balance point, one hand gripped over and one under..."

Lessons followed that taxed both Khalidah's patience and endurance. Gadil forced her to step into the thrust over and over until her body followed his commands of its own. Muscles hardened from a lifetime of labor crumbled under the exercise. The backs of her legs ached with threatening cramps, and she rubbed them beside the fire convinced Gadil would not have stopped if the sky had not darkened.

"Tell me a story," Khalidah said.

"I am no bard." Gadil held the spear in the fire and watched the wood blacken.

"I'm too tired to fall asleep. At least tell me why we are going after this dragon."

"Because it exists."

"Dog balls. If that's the only answer you can muster, then I'll pack up and return to my master now."

Gadil fixed her with a stare but clearly recognized the truth of her words. He sighed, closed his eyes, and breathed deeply.

"In the days before he created men," Gadil said, eyes still closed, "Dend watched over the land with his child, Dendia, circling in the sky."

"This sounds like scripture."

"It is, though I am condensing the story. A full telling would involve a day and a night, with many prayers and dances."

"I see."

"Dend loved Dendia above all things," said Gadil, his eyes open but inwardly focused, "and shone all his love upon him. Then one day the Great Wyrm came upon the child when Dend was turned away and bit him. Dend discovered the Great Wyrm and cast him down to the land, but its poison was already at work. The child weakened and died. Dend cried a rain of tears that flooded the land. At last he created men so that they could hunt the Great Wyrm and all its offspring. I am the Wearer of the Blade, the embodiment of Dend's retribution on the land. All of the Great Wyrm's creations are to be slain."

"I suppose there are more than just dragons perched in that family tree." Khalidah sipped at some honeyed water.

"Dragons are the most mature form. Snakes, lizards, crocodiles...I am vowed to slay all of the Great Wyrm's children."

"Snakes are not a younger form of dragon. Neither are crocodiles. They are separate species."

"Dend commands me." Gadil spoke with unshakeable firmness.

Khalidah watched a small movement at the edge of the firelight. Attracted by the warmth, a small grass snake slithered nearer.

"That will turn into a dragon?" she asked.

Brilliant steel flashed across the flames, like a star's twinkling. Gadil drew the sword back and slid it into its sheath. The snake's two halves wriggled slowly and stilled.

"Not anymore," Gadil said. He lay down and closed his eyes.

Two weeks of riding and training with the spear turned Khalidah's muscles from apprentice-smooth to stone-hard. While they still burned in the morning, she amazed herself frequently by running a hand over her abaya and feeling the strength underneath. Particularly different was her stomach; she could feel hard ridges where before it had been soft and flat.

"It happens quickly," said Gadil. Khalidah dropped her arms back to the reins. Gadil was looking at her over his shoulder. "The physical transformation. If we were at the temple's facility the difference would be even more dramatic."

"I don't feel this kind of talk is appropriate," she said.

"Why not?"

"Men and women should not speak to each other of their bodies."

"Your actions belie your modesty. Were you not aware that yesterday morning you stopped raising your veil in my presence?"

Khalidah reached up and brushed her fingertips over her bare chin and cheek. She quickly lifted the veil and hooked it in place.

"I apologize, Gadil," she said softly, almost meekly.

"None needed. We are partners on this adventure. If it is more comfortable for you to have your veil lowered while we travel, I will think nothing less of you for it. Besides, it makes it easier for me to tell when you are insulting me." He smiled at her, and she returned it. "You are more than I thought you would be. Women I have known have all been weak-willed, like broken horses, subject only to the whip and saddle. I apologize for putting you in the same category."

"No apology necessary."

"Yes, it is. I saw you with Samien, how you bent at his feet. Every woman I have ever known has done that."

"He is my master, my teacher. I would act the same if he were a woman."

"I understand." Gadil put force into his words. "I apologize."

"Accepted. Will you teach me to use a sword?" Her eyes never left the tern's-egg pommel as she spoke.

"No." One word, without inflection.

"Why not?"

Gadil turned in his saddle.

"I already said there is not enough time to teach you even the most rudimentary passes. But if we were back at the temple training grounds I would still make the attempt. Here, the only sword I have is the Blade, and you cannot touch it."

"Is it a crime against your god?" Khalidah knew that was not the reason, yet Gadil seemed reluctant to continue.

"There is nothing in the texts that says another may not touch the Blade. It is merely fact. I am the Wearer, and should another touch the Blade they would be stricken by Dend's might. Many thieves have been found in the temple burned to cinders."

"From only touching the sword?"

"Yes, from only touching it. Dend's wrath is strong. None but the proclaimed Wearer may handle it."

Khalidah looked again at the sword then blinked her eyes to begin a deep seeing. A bright spot glowed on the blade a few fingers from the handle. It grew quickly until nothing but white covered her eyes. She felt herself falling and cared for only the beautiful music that filled her ears and the white poetry that blinded her.

Water splashed her face. Gadil knelt over her with a soaked cloth clutched in his fist.

"Are you well?" he asked.

"I think so." Khalidah blinked. She shuddered as she gasped for air.

"As I said, Dend.'s might carries a sharp edge."

Khalidah nodded.

A shadow flashed across the sky, like a hurried cloud. Khalidah's horse whinnied nearby. It snorted panic and galloped off. Gadil turned to look over his shoulder, but the thing above them was gone.

"We leave the horses here," he said. "The forest will provide us cover until we climb above the timberline. After that, we will use caution. If, that is, you are finished with your little rest."

Gadil held his hand out as he smiled. Khalidah took it and regained her feet, though she felt no desire to lift the corners of her mouth. It had been a huge shadow.

Khalidah handed the spyglass back to Gadil, and he pushed it closed until it fit inside the hard, leather pouch on his belt.

"We will climb the north side of the mountain," he said. "The horses can stay here. They are not so stupid as to venture about. Then we will look for a secondary entrance to its lair, one that is too small for it but will permit passage to us."

"Its lair? How do you know the lair is nearby?"

"This is not my first dragon hunt, Khalidah. They do not sun themselves away from their homes. Once full of heat, they will sleep. If we can use stealth to near the Black Dragon while it naps, its death may come more swiftly."

"We should speak of your tactics." Gadil walked brazenly through the forest, comfortable that the evergreen trees concealed them. Khalidah constantly looked behind and above her, seeing nothing but tree-broken sky.

"That would be a complicated discussion. My tactics will depend on the actions of the dragon." He stepped over a fallen log. Khalidah thought it merely an interruption, but it became apparent after a long moment that he was done speaking.

"I want to plan tactics of my own, Gadil. The last thing I want to do is create a manipulation that does more harm to you than the dragon."

"It is all I can tell you." With that, there was no doubt he was done.

The tree line broke again. Khalidah looked nervously at a wide patch of open terrain, separated by a trickling stream. Loose stone littered the ground. In the majesty of the mountain and the looming presence of the giant beast somewhere above them, Khalidah felt as if she had shrunk and the stones were dust particles. She wanted to summon a small bit of Essence to remind her of the power she controlled. The dragon would sense it, so she swallowed her fear and felt small.

By contrast, Gadil never paused. He marched straight across the clearing.

Once, she saw him look up. Perhaps it was out of nervousness. Perhaps he saw some small bit of movement that eluded her. Certainly nothing bothered them as they stepped over the stream, crossed the clearing, and began the arduous climb up the rough slope.

A gentle bowl of weed-filled rock greeted them after not too long a climb.

"I see we are on the right path," Gadil said, continuing up without pause, hand over hand. When Khalidah reached the lip of the bowl, she saw bones. Stripped of flesh, cracked by powerful jaws, the collection of deer, cattle and lesser beasts seemed both intentionally piled and randomly strewn.

"It pushes them from its lair," said Khalidah to Gadil's back. "Like an owl."

"Yes. A dragon's lair is as barren as a dried well. They all disdain clutter."

"How orderly." She stretched for a handhold and found one foot dangling before she regained her grip. With head pressed against the cool rock face, she inhaled deeply. "You say the lair is empty?"

"As a grave." His voice was distant.

"There is no treasure hoard?"

"I have yet to see one, though some dragons collect shiny objects the way ravens do. Would you like some assistance?"

Khalidah raised a hand and grabbed at another section of the steep incline.

"Just catching my breath," she said. It was probably her imagination that made her think Gadil had frowned again, for surely the grimace would have made no sound. She looked up in time to see both his feet come away from the wall.

For an instant, she thought he was floating. Then he grunted and hauled himself into an opening, his legs and feet disappearing in fits as if the mountain swallowed him in gradual gulps.

Khalidah climbed the rest of the way and felt for purchase. The tunnel entrance was smooth from a lifetime of discarded skeletons and perching talons. She couldn't get a grip. Fingers scrabbling, her feet threatened to loose themselves from the tiny ledge that held them. In a moment she knew she would fall.

"Gadil!"

His hand appeared and grabbed her kitten-like by the scruff of her robes. As easily as if she were fastened to a bricklayer's harness, she rose. Above the edge, Gadil lay on his belly, one powerful arm pressed against the wall. She clambered into the tunnel. Without doubt, she knew he could have lifted her the entire way and set her down with a butterfly's grace.

Gadil sat up while Khalidah panted. From the bag slung over his shoulder he drew an oil lantern. It sparked to life with the turning of a wheel.

"Not exactly the Great Lighthouse, is it?" she said.

"Your eyes will adjust."

"I could make more light. It is a very small Weaving."

"The dragon will sense it. Should we catch the beast in post-sunning lethargy it will be far easier to dispatch than if we signal our approach."

Gadil stood and walked confidently into the darkness.

"It better be napping," Khalidah muttered. "We're going to trip over the thing." She untied the spear from her back and held it out, point down. The reassuring taps of its tip against the floor dispelled the notion that she was about to fall into a ravine better than Gadil's bobbing oil lamp did. When she glanced over her shoulder, the winding tunnel had erased the light of the cavern entrance.

Quick as lightning bugs winking out, the dragon attacked. Two hisses, indiscernible from one another: scale against stone and steel against sheath. The oil lamp dropped to the cavern floor, jerked as it bounced, and lost its flame.

Khalidah felt the dragon's presence as if she were running her hand over its hide. It reeked of carrion flesh. Air moved away from it like it was repelled by its shape. Something—the tip of a tightly furled wing, the end of its whip-like tail—sliced the air just before her face like an executioner's blade.

Gadil grunted with strain. The dragon spat. Their bodies danced noisily in the utter blackness. Khalidah lifted her spear, thought of impaling Gadil in the dark, and held it before her as if she marched with the Shah's banner in a parade.

A wall of muscle sent her flying. Jaw clamped, she awaited the cavern wall's impact and found it just as unyielding as she anticipated. Light flashed, and she believed the dragon had loosed its flame until the pain coursed through her head and neck. More brightness winked inside her eyelids. She dropped to the stone floor, the wooden haft of her spear clattering nearby.

A basso rumbling was either Gadil or the dragon. An ugly slicing sound prefaced the dragon's howling. A second and third, metal through flesh, and Khalidah felt the dragon flinch with an opening wide of its body. A taloned foot stamped in the darkness beside Khalidah's face, wind-blown pebbles scoring the skin of her hands and arms. Gadil grunted again, clearly in pain. The ringing of his sword against the cavern floor sounded like a death toll.

His footsteps leapt, a mouse's frantic escaping. The dragon's jaws snapped together with empty futility.

Khalidah felt for the spear in the dark and lifted it. As the wood scraped against stone, she heard the dragon shift its bulk toward her.

Teeth slammed together before her face, spittle spattering her. The spear jarred like the mountain itself had grabbed it, and the dragon howled, bowling her back with its breath. It exhaled again, this time with far less force. The spear, pinned against the wall behind her and held upright by an invisible force, vibrated in her hands. It pulled from her grip as the dragon's bulk settled.

No less fetid, air escaped the dragon's mouth in a long, flowing exhale, like an air bladder punctured by a seamstress' needle.

Her mind spun, flickering will-o-wisps still dancing before her eyes. She tried the illumination Weaving and lost focus. She lowered herself to hands and knees and felt for the lamp.

First it was nothing but rock floor she touched. Her hand brushed against a wall of smooth, overlapping layers, very hard like the stone itself. A puddle of warm liquid splashed as she set her palm squarely in it. She moved around the dead dragon and continued to search.

"Stop!"

Gadil's command froze her with fear. His voice was to her right, echoing with the kind of resolve that demanded to be obeyed.

"If you touch the Blade," he said, "you will die. I will find the lamp." She heard him crawling around, eventually moving something supremely hard and metallic. The sword slid into his sheath, and he continued his search. Another metal object clattered, softer and hollow. He turned the wheel, sparks flew, and the lamp blazed to life in the Stygian black.

The dragon was huge, lying on its side. Khalidah's spear pierced its throat at the base of the neck, the tip penetrating out the scales of the upper back. She hadn't seen its head before; round and triangular, it reminded her of a viper. Two delicate goat's horns stuck straight out of the brow. A flat, not very long tongue hung from a mouth filled with tiny, knifepoint teeth.

"You were correct to hold your magic," said Gadil. "The Black Dragon would have undoubtedly detected it this close to her lair."

"This is not the Black Dragon?" Khalidah asked, voice cracking.

"It is her offspring. Two and a half, perhaps three years old. It would have been ready to leave the nest at the end of the season. It is fine that you slew it. Well done."

Khalidah let her gaze drift over the infant dragon fully four times her length from snout to tail. Even with Gadil's great frame beside it, the dead beast still looked huge.

"We must hurry," he said. "Should she scent this hatchling's death we will lose our opportunity for surprise."

And the Black Dragon attacked.

It enveloped the cavern with its size, like a tidal surge. One moment Gadil and Khalidah stood in the emptiness of the tunnel; the next, there was nothing but dragon. She was wrong to think of the first dragon as huge. With the mother surrounding them, it was clearly a pup.

A great head snapped forward, jaws closing with the sound of slamming dungeon doors. Gadil had been there, and suddenly he wasn't. His sword glinted in the light of the fallen lamp. Two fast slashes sounded weak and ineffective, but the dragon roared with furious injury. The breath of it pinned Khalidah to the wall.

It turned away from her to pursue Gadil. The dragon's hind leg stamped the floor beside Khalidah. She could have reached out and touched it, caressed the overlapping scales that looked like a butterfly's shimmering colors examined in the magnifying lenses. Then it pounced away. The bulk of its tail slammed into the wall like a battering ram against a portcullis. Debris rained down on Khalidah. Another step of the gargantuan leg and the lantern went out again.

Khalidah lifted her arms and sprayed the walls with light. In the brightness of two suns, the beast flinched. Metal struck flesh, the dragon roared and pounced, and Khalidah caught a fleeting glimpse of Gadil's blur as he retreated from his attack. The dragon hissed in frustration or pain and snapped its jaws again over nothing but air.

The Weaving came to her hand as if by itself, uninvited and clamoring for attention. The energy burned in her palm. She hurled it at the dragon's flank. Invisible to anyone's eyes but hers, Khalidah watched in horror as the blasting deflected harmlessly, a stone skipping on a lake. It shot into the wall and tore the rock apart.

The mountain itself complained, its agony echoing through the long tunnels. Shards of stone flew in all directions. Khalidah crossed her forearms before her face and begged for a shielding that never came. Flecks cut her skin; a larger chunk of debris punched her in the belly, taking her air. She fell to hands and knees into the puddle of the dragonling's blood.

Dripping gore from the rocky shrapnel, the dragon's head moved with evermore-furious haste. Gadil slipped to the side, into the dragon's now blind left. His sword bit deep into the shoulder joint and stuck in the bone. The dragon bent its snake-like neck nearly double and closed its mouth before Gadil. His back was to her, but his paralysis spoke volumes. He twisted as he crumpled to the floor, his ribcage torn completely away. The Blade struck the cavern floor: simple, unmoving steel.

The dragon spat out Gadil's torso and locked its gaze on Khalidah. Saliva and blood dripped from its mouth. It inhaled briefly and roared, filling her with horror. Bits of meat struck her face and clung to her hair.

She rose to her knees and pressed her palms out. The force of her Weaving slid her backwards. Cascades of brilliant, musical light poured from her and onto the dragon mere paces away. It would have destroyed every tree in an oasis forest. The Weaving crumbled as it touched the monster, falling away like windblown sand.

The dragon lifted its head and inhaled, much deeper than before. It pulled its wings tight to its body, head high. Beyond the terrifying beast, Khalidah saw the glittering of precious stones stashed in a crevice that indeed reminded her of a raven's collection of shiny bits. It was the last thing she thought of before the dragon emptied its flame sac upon her.

It vomited flames onto the invader before it could bite and slash like the other one had. Content with the stench of charred flesh in its nostrils, the dragon reared back its head and poured the last of its flames out in a triumphant roar. Movement brought its attention back to the dead thing, which was not as dead as it first looked. Stripped of meat, it was more than bones: bright shiny surface like a sun-reflected lake. It was still vaguely shaped like an invader and moved toward the dragon on its hind legs. The beast's head snapped forward, jaws wide. The shiny invader lifted its hands and stopped the dragon's head as if it had been sealed in amber. A twist, some snapped vertebrae, and the dragon fell lifeless. Beyond it, revealed in the still-glowing magical light, shone a nest of raw gemstones and crystal. At the feet of the humanoid thing lay a dead warrior and his sword. The thing bent down and grasped the Blade's handle.

Samien raised himself out of the chair and shuffled to the edge of the porch. The springtime rains were long overdue, and the arriving horses kicked up a cloud of fine dust that choked him. He coughed into a handkerchief, throat rattling.

The Malek's youngest son dismounted with little fanfare. Though his traveling clothes were fine, he bore them with no apparent concern for the influence of their cut or color.

Samien bowed.

"Sahib al-Mamlaka," he said, coughing only once into his handkerchief.

"Please," said the prince, an honest-sounding word, "I abhor such trappings. My two eldest brothers can squabble over those trivialities. If you must, 'Prince Awaan,' though I would prefer you left off the honorific."

"As you wish, Awaan." Great coughs clutched Samien, and he bent with cloth over his mouth. His hand blindly found the porch railing. Awaan stepped forward and lifted both arms to keep Samien from tumbling to the ground.

"My wife is plagued at this time of year as well," he said. "I suspect it is some kind of reaction to the budding trees and their annoying golden dust."

"It is more than that, I fear. I know it has been only a few short months since our last correspondence, but the disease of the wasting lungs has come to me. There is no possibility of my joining your adventure."

Awaan put his hands on his hips, his face screwed into troubling thought. He looked over his shoulder at the caravan of swordsmen and assistants.

"The investment in this campaign is extensive, Samien. Bilisi is the most powerful of the shayatin. We need sorcery to foil this demon; steel will be insufficient. It is the demon's hoard of gold that will allow me to break free of the royal yoke."

"The journey would kill me, Awaan," said Samien.

A long pause followed in which the warrior-prince held his lips together tightly and shook his head often.

"Then we must return," he said with finality. "What is one more failure in the eyes of my father?"

"Perhaps there is an option," Samien said as Awaan turned away. The prince stopped and focused tenuous hope back at him.

"If it is sound, speak it."

"The shayatin are notoriously resistant to Weavings, great and small. It is your blades that will bring it down. My contribution would be only to subvert the traps and minions along the way."

Khalidah stepped onto the porch and adjusted her veil in time to hear, "My apprentice could go in my stead. I'm sure she would prove most useful."

About The Author

Robert J. Santa has been writing speculative fiction for more than thirty years. His works have appeared in numerous print and online venues. Robert lives in Rhode Island, USA, with his beautiful wife and two equally beautiful daughters.

CONFESSIONS

BY FREDRICK OBERMEYER

Detective Ivan Kostokis was typing up an arrest report on his computer when a chubby, balding man in a gray trenchcoat came into the squad room of the ninety-third precinct in Brooklyn. He was carrying a large tan briefcase.

"Are you in charge here?" the man said.

"No, my lieutenant's out at the moment. But I'm Detective Kostokis, and I can help you, Mr..."

He looked around furtively, then sat in a chair next to Kostokis's desk and said, "Harold Martins. I work as an investment banker down at Morton and Fielding."

"How can I help you, Mr. Martins?"

"I'm the Sheepshead Bay Butcher, and I want to confess all of my crimes."

Great, another crank, Kostokis thought.

Before Kostokis could say anything further, Martins opened the case, took out a plastic-wrapped serrated knife, hacksaw and a cleaver and dropped it on Kostokis's desk; the plastic around all the implements was covered in dried blood. Then he laid down several Polaroids of butchered women, a smartphone and a paper map of Brooklyn with several red circles in and around Sheepshead Bay.

Kostokis stared in utter shock. The police and FBI had been trying to clear the Sheepshead case for nearly a year with no luck. Now the killer just waltzed in and dumped the whole case right in his lap.

"Hold it right there!" Kostokis said.

The detective burst out of his chair, drew the Glock 19 pistol from his belt holster and pointed it at Martins. The other detectives in the room drew their own guns and pointed them at Martins.

"Don't shoot!" Martins said, throwing his hands up. "I give up!"

"Down on the floor with your hands behind your head!" Kostokis said. "Now!"

Martins complied with the command immediately. As soon as he was

51

down, Kostokis and the other detectives converged on the banker.

Kostokis holstered his Glock and frisked Martins for other weapons. Finding none, he cuffed Martins and pulled the man to his feet.

"Easy!" Martins said. "I just want to confess!"

"All right, Mr. Martins. We'll take you into the interrogation room and you can tell us what you want there."

"Okay."

Kostokis led the handcuffed into the dingy, olive green room with another detective and sat him down behind a gray table. A few minutes later, a third detective brought in a digital recorder and Kostokis pressed record. He gave the date and time and informed Martins of his Miranda rights, which he acknowledged.

"Do you wish to have an attorney present during questioning, Mr. Martins?" Kostokis said.

"No. I...I'm sick, and I need help. Look, I'll sign anything you want me to. Just put me away before I hurt any more women. Please."

"Why are you confessing now?"

"I don't know why. I just felt like it was the right thing to do." He frowned. "What, you don't want me to confess?"

"No, I want you to confess. It just isn't typical."

"This isn't typical for me either. Until yesterday I didn't tell anybody about what I did. Then suddenly, I

don't know what happened, but I felt this urgent need to confess."

"Okay, Mr. Martins. We'll get the DA down here and you can tell us the whole story."

A knock came at the door.

"Yeah?" Kostokis said, shutting off the recorder.

The desk sergeant for the nine-three, Bill Covel, came into the interrogation room with a young teen who had green spiky hair and huge gauged earrings.

"Detective?" Covel said.

"One second, Bill."

"We got this kid here, claims he wants to confess to stealing some iPhones out of Korpal's Electronics last week."

"Okay, Bill, get Sal on it. I'm kind of busy here."

"That's not all."

Kostokis frowned. "What? Does somebody else want to confess?"

"Yeah."

"Who?"

Covel gestured behind him and said, "About a hundred other people."

"You're shitting me."

"See for yourself."

The detective walked out of the interrogation room and over to the stairwell, looked down to the first floor of the precinct and gawked at all the people milling around down there.

"This is going to be a long night," Kostokis said.

Even with several of the squad's other detectives called back in, Kostokis could only handle so many people at a time. While he worked, even more confessors came into the precinct and the phones began ringing off the hook.

Despite the extra staff, the squad room quickly turned into a madhouse.

After twelve hours, Kostokis had to quit from sheer exhaustion. But the squad cleared nearly three hundred cases in that time.

When asked why they confessed, everybody gave the same answer.

They didn't know why. They just felt they had to do it.

What is causing all these people to confess? Kostokis thought. Did somebody put something in the water?

Feeling every second of his fifty-three years on Earth, Kostokis trudged home to his apartment. He was so tired that he didn't even bother to say hello to his wife, Deborah.

Instead he poured himself a glass of ouzo on ice, marveling as the liquor turned from clear to milky when it touched the cubes.

As a child, his grandmother used to speak to him in Greek in her small apartment garden while she let him watch the ouzo turn white, which always fascinated him. Sometimes she would even let him have a small sip of the fiery liquid when nobody was around.

How long has she been gone? Kostokis thought wistfully. Thirty years?

He sipped the ouzo, then crashed on the couch and immediately fell asleep.

Sometime later, Deborah shook him awake.

Kostokis leaned up, rubbed his aching neck and glanced right. The clock across from him said it was just past eleven A.M.

"Hey," Kostokis said. "You just get home from work?"

Frowning, Deborah shook her head and said, "No, I've been here for a little while."

"What's wrong?"

"Ivan, I'm going out for a while. But first I have to confess something."

"Not you too." He sighed. "We already had a bunch of people at the station confessing last night."

"Really?"

"Yeah." He shook his head. "Christ, whole fucking world's going crazy out there. Like it's Judgment Day or something."

"Ivan—"

"Look, whatever it is, just forget about it, okay?"

"I can't just forget about it. I've been carrying this thing around for years."

"Deb, please, these past few hours I heard enough confessions to last me a lifetime—"

"Jenny Hoffner."

"Huh?"

"She was my best friend in high school."

"What about her?"

"I killed her."

"Deb—"

"Please, I need to tell somebody!"

Kostokis groaned, figuring she was going to talk no matter what he said. So he gestured for her to continue.

"One winter we were ice skating by ourselves on Lake Pallard and she, she broke through the ice. And she started screaming 'Debbie, Debbie, help me!'"

Deborah burst into tears. "I don't know what came over me then. There was a branch nearby and I could've saved her. But I...I just stared at her."

"Jesus Christ," Kostokis said.

"I was angry with her, you see. She was always more popular than me and the kids always called me braceface and dumped shit in my hair. But then one day I heard Jenny making fun of me with Ann Carter behind my back. I....I felt so betrayed. And now here she was helpless..." Deborah sniffed, tears streaking her mascara. "And I just let her drown."

Silence passed for a moment; Kostokis stared at his wife like she was a stranger.

"I remember afterwards I faked some tears, ran back home and had my dad come down to the lake with the neighbors." She looked past Kostokis. "They said it wasn't my fault. But it was."

A sick feeling tightened Kostokis' stomach.

"It was an accident, Deb. You got scared and panicked—"

"No, don't you see? I pushed her onto the thin ice and she fell through!"

Kostokis could only blink. After ten years of marriage to his third wife, he thought he knew Deborah pretty well. But it seemed he didn't really know her at all.

"Do you know what the worst thing is?" She laughed bitterly. "Up until yesterday, I didn't feel the least bit bad about it. Hell, I was glad the fucking bitch was dead."

"Honey, don't say another word. Go see a priest and tell him what you did."

"No, I want you to take me to the station and have them arrest me."

Stunned, Kostokis gaped at his wife. "Are you crazy? I can't arrest my own wife for murder."

"Ivan, please."

"I don't fucking believe this." He rubbed his forehead. "I suppose you can't remember why you're confessing either."

"No." Deborah frowned. "But I do remember one thing."

"What?"

"I was walking someplace."

"Where?"

"Central Park, I think."

"Where in Central Park?"

"I don't know. But whatever happened, I think it happened there."

"Are you sure?" Kostokis said. "Nobody else remembered anything."

"Yes, I think so."

Deborah gripped Kostokis's hand.

"Do you still love me?" she said.

"Of course I do." He raised her hand to his lips and kissed it.

"I'm a good person, aren't I? I mean, I did a bad thing in the past, but I'm not really evil, am I?"

"We've all done bad things, honey."

She pulled her hand away from him. "I'm going to the police."

Kostokis bolted up and grabbed her. "Don't do this, Deb! At least go talk to a lawyer before you do something you can't take back."

"If you won't come with me, then fine. I'll go alone."

"Honey, they'll lock you up if you confess. I might not be able to help you."

"I don't care anymore." She hugged him tight. "I love you."

"I love you too, but think about this. Please!"

She let him go. "I have thought about it, and I need to do this."

She kissed him on the cheek and slid out the door.

"Deb, wait!"

He chased her out of the apartment, but by the time he got to the elevator the doors had closed. Wheezing, Kostokis rushed down eight flights of stairs, his big belly slowing him down. By the time he arrived at the lobby, though, she was long gone. Worn out, Kostokis collapsed in a nearby chair, trying to catch his breath.

"Fuck!" Kostokis said.

He considered chasing her, but what good would it do? She hadn't told him which precinct she was going to. Besides, it was her life. Short of tying her up, he couldn't stop her from confessing.

As he caught his breath, something she said popped back into his mind.

Central Park.

Maybe I can find some answers there, Kostokis thought.

A half-hour later, Kostokis entered Central Park. Unsure of what to look for, his eyes kept darting back and forth between the walkway and the trees. The snow and cold had driven away most of the people and only a few passed by. Along the way, he tried calling the nine-three and police dispatch to see if Deborah was there. But all the lines were busy, so he pocketed his smartphone and kept looking.

Nothing seemed out of the ordinary, though, and Kostokis wondered if Deborah had lost her mind.

Ten minutes later, he came upon an old homeless man sitting by himself on a park bench. He was bundled up in several jackets and pairs of pants, his breath misting in the world; a black New York Yankees ball cap stood atop his head, and he had a grizzled face with white stubble. The rotten onion stink of his body odor was so strong that it made Kostokis's eyes water even from a distance.

Kostokis had seen so many homeless people throughout his career that he barely took notice of the man, except for his smell. But as he passed, the man said, "Hey, you're a cop, right?"

Kostokis stopped, turned to the bum and said, "Yeah."

"I knew it. Moment I saw ya, I knew it. You got that cop look."

Kostokis glanced around. It was quiet, the light snow falling silently. "You see anything funny around here these past few days?"

The old man chuckled and said, "In Central Park? What isn't funny around here?"

"True enough."

"You got a smoke?"

"Sorry. I quit a few years back."

"Hey, you want to see something?"

Kostokis swallowed hard, wondering if the guy was a weenie wagger.

"No thanks."

"It'll just take a moment, Detective Kostokis."

A sudden chill passed up his spine.

"How'd you know my name?"

The bum lunged at Kostokis and pressed his dirty, gnarled fingers against the detective's face. Kostokis tried to push free, but his mind quickly plummeted into a dark abyss.

When Kostokis awoke, he found himself lying on green grass. He staggered to his feet and gasped as he found himself standing in an enormous grassy field. It was a sunny day, the sky full of white clouds. In the distance there lay a large red and white barn and a plain brown, two-story house.

The bum was standing across from him, wearing the same outfit as he had in the park.

"What's going on?" Kostokis said.

"My name is Stanley Misenkar," the bum said. "And I've formed a telepathic link with your mind."

"I..." Kostokis blinked.

"That's me as a child."

Stanley pointed across the field to a small boy with sandy blond hair dressed in denim overalls. A glowing green stone lay in the center of the wide open area.

"When I was eight years old, I discovered that stone in a field outside my grandparents' farm in Havenwood, Connecticut," Stanley said.

The boy tried to pick it up and howled as it burnt him. He dropped the rock and clutched his hand. Kostokis cringed and glanced at old Stanley. The bum took off his right glove and revealed burn scars on his palm and fingers.

Moments later, the boy screamed and swung his foot back to kick the stone. But a second later, he stopped. The green glow faded from the rock. A curious look appeared on his face. He grabbed a stick and poked the rock, then carefully touched the edge again with a finger and drew it back.

This time it didn't burn him.

"The stone gave me the power to call anyone to me or drive them away," Stanley said. "And once they were near, I could enter their minds simply by touching them. After that, I could make them do anything I wanted."

A white flash blinded Kostokis for a moment, then he found himself in a green-walled study full of old books and a roaring fireplace. A teenaged Stanley was touching the right cheek of an old man with his scarred hand and whispering into his ear.

The man's eyes were glazed.

After Stanley spoke, the man took out several stacks of hundreds from his desk and gave them to the teenager, who eagerly shoved them into a satchel.

"Now the gun," young Stanley said.

The man grabbed a snubnose revolver out of the desk, stuck it in his mouth and squeezed the trigger. Kostokis yelped as the man's brains painted the wall behind him red.

Stunned, he stumbled back, turned and found himself drifting down an endless brown oak-paneled hallway with Stanley hovering beside him. Several doors were open on both sides.

In one doorway, a naked man raped a young woman in the back of a car. In another, a fat woman strangled a child in a gravel pit. In a third, a young boy set his sleeping parents on fire. In a fourth, a businessman dumped a bag full of diamonds into the hands of a now adult Stanley.

Kostokis gawked at the numerous doorways flew by faster and became a blur.

"I could make anybody do anything I want," Stanley said. "After a while, I lost count as to how many lives I destroyed."

"Why do this?" Kostokis said.

"Because I wanted money and power and the stone gave me the means to acquire both."

The hallway abruptly ended with another flash of white light and Kostokis found himself in a church during a wedding. Stanley was at the altar, kissing a beautiful young blond-haired woman.

"I only stopped after I married my wife, Sharon," Stanley said.

Kostokis swallowed hard, his stomach roiling.

"I tried to be a good husband and father and not use the stone."

The scene shifted to an enormous egg-blue walled mansion living room with Sharon, her belly now swollen, holding a baby. Stanley cooed at the child, but again the scene shifted to a kitchen where a young boy and girl were screaming their heads off.

Stanley's face reddened with rage as Sharon said, "Take care of the god-damned kids yourself, Stan!"

"Alas, I failed." He waved his hand and they were back in the living room. His wife and children were sitting on the couch, and they had the same glazed look as the old man in the study.

"They annoyed me so much with their whining that I made them behave."

Trembling, Kostokis turned on Stanley, wanting to punch Stanley.

"How could you do this to your own family?"

"It was easy." Stanley bowed his head. "For a while, things were perfect. In fact, they were too perfect."

The living room morphed into a patio with an enormous backyard full of hedge animals lying beyond. Stanley was sitting at a glass breakfast table with his family, holding the stone; the expressions of his family were glazed and they smiled vacantly.

"Sweetheart?" Stanley said to his daughter.

"Yes, Daddy?"

"Smack your head into the table."

His daughter smashed her head into the table, cracking the glass. The family continued to stare impassively as his daughter blinked dazedly and leaned up, blood trickling down her forehead. She was still smiling, as was Stanley.

"Again," Stanley said.

She whammed her head into it again, nearly shattering the glass.

"The rest of you, smack your heads too."

His wife and son smacked their heads into the glass and shattered it, then leaned up smiling, bits of glass stuck in their heads, blood leaking down their faces.

"May I go play in the yard, Daddy?" the little girl said, the red reaching her neck and staining her pink satin dress.

"Of course, sweetheart," Stanley said.

He kissed his daughter's head wound and licked the blood off his lips as she staggered away.

Sharon smiled, her expression still vacuous as her wounds bled freely.

The hairs on the back of Kostokis's neck stood.

"I grew tired of my rich, perfect life and wanted to shatter it to pieces,"

Stanley said. "I could have so easily made Sharon kill the kids and then herself. But at that point, I felt the rock made things too easy. I..." His voice wavered. "It was like a game to me. I wanted to kill them and get away with it without using the rock."

"No," Kostokis said.

"I planned the crime for five months."

"I don't want to see—"

Kostokis shuddered as he found himself in a children's bedroom with giraffes and pink balloons on the wallpaper. Sharon was reading a bedtime story to the children. As she turned the page, Stanley came into the room. He was wearing earplugs and holding a Browning Auto-5 shotgun.

"Stanley, what are you—!"

He fired and her head exploded into red mist. Spattered with their mother's blood and brains, the children screamed and cowered on their beds. Stanley's face twisted with savage delight as he turned the shotgun on his kids and fired one shot into each of them.

After the last shot, images strobed in Kostokis's mind.

Stanley ranksacking money and other valuables from his own mansion. Stanley breaking a window on the patio door and leaving it open. Stanley wiping down the prints on the shotgun, then throwing it and the bag full of loot into a nearby lake in the dead of night. Stanley wailing to the police in his living room, saying, "How could they do this to my babies?"

Enraged, Kostokis tried to lunge at Stanley, but the older man held up his hand. The detective froze in space, as did the scene.

"How could you..."

"Yes, I was a monster," Stanley said. "And for a while, I thought I was going to get away with it. But then the police found a witness who claimed to see me flee my home on the night of the murders." His lower lip quivered. "In a way, I was glad, though. I wanted to go before a jury and get away with my crime completely."

The living room shifted to sometime later; a detective slapped handcuffs on Stanley. Then the mansion faded to reveal a courtroom. The jury entered the box and a judge banged his gavel. Kostokis spun around and found himself staring at Stanley, smiling at the defense table. But time accelerated and the smile changed into a nervous frown.

"Fear got the better of me," Stanley said. "So like a coward, I cheated."

The courtroom faded to reveal a weedy field at night, the full moon glowing overhead. Stanley was holding the glowing stone and the jury members were standing at the edge of the field with a US marshal.

One by one, Stanley mindtouched them.

"Not guilty," the foreman said behind Kostokis.

Suddenly free, Kostokis turned and found himself back in the courtroom. Shock tightened the faces of the prosecution and press, but Stanley stood beaming.

"I had won," Stanley said. "And thanks to double jeopardy, they couldn't try me again."

The sound of crying suddenly filled the air. Kostokis blinked and found himself inside a yacht cabin. Now with his blond hair mostly gray, Stanley sat weeping by himself on the cabin bed, clutching a portrait of his family.

"Considering what a vicious person I was, I should've been happy," Stanley said. "Yet over the following decades guilt began to eat away at me. I stopped using the rock and tried to live a quiet life."

The moment froze.

"Then about a year ago, I got the bad news."

The cabin turned into a doctor's office. An old doctor looked gravely at a crestfallen, white-haired Stanley, sitting on a paper-covered table.

"I'm sorry, Mr. Misenkar," the doctor said. "You have terminal congestive heart failure."

Stanley shifted from the business suit he was wearing to his bum outfit and the doctor disappeared.

"Needless to say, I was shocked," Stanley said. "And I suddenly became afraid that I would burn in hell for all my sins. So I tried to make amends."

More images filled Kostokis's mind. Stanley stuffing a wad of cash onto a church plate. Movers carrying furniture past a "FOR SALE" sign outside his mansion.

"I liquidated my entire fortune, gave it to charity and decided to live as a bum in Central Park."

Kostokis turned and found himself back in Central Park with Stanley begging for change next to a tree.

"It wasn't enough, though," Stanley said. "I had to confess my sins to somebody, so I used the stone on some random guy."

A short red-haired guy appeared next to a tree. Stanley touched the man's cheek and Kostokis heard a child weeping.

"And I learned that prick was molesting his seven year old daughter," Stanley said, grimacing. "I was so disgusted that I made him confess."

The man shifted into a woman wearing a mink stole.

"Then I found another woman who shot her husband and his mistress and was never caught," Stanley said. "I made her confess too."

More images of Stanley touching people's faces flashed through his mind.

"So many unpunished criminals like me walked the streets that I began to fear I wouldn't find one decent person in this whole stinking city. Eventually, I grew so tired of their sins on top of my own that I let the rest go for the time being and simply kept a mental tab on them."

The last person disappeared and revealed Stanley keeling over on a green park bench.

"Then one day I got a bad pain in my chest."

A moment later, he leaned up.

"I was so scared I was dying, though thankfully the pain went away." He frowned. "But at that moment, I decided 'fuck it.' I'll make them all confess and do something good with my life before I die."

He took out the stone from his pocket, clutched it tight in his hands and closed his eyes.

"I used the stone to call the people I already mindtouched back to the park and make others leave so there wouldn't be a crowd."

One by one, people showed up in front of Stanley, and he mindtouched each one. Deborah appeared among the large group of thousands of confessors.

"Even that wasn't enough, though," Stanley said. "I want someone who will make other criminals confess after I die." He looked into Kostokis's eyes. "That's why I had your wife drop you some hints to see if you would come here on your own. If you didn't, I would've used the stone to bring you here eventually. But in any case, I need a good man to continue my work and your wife's memories showed me your goodness."

"How can you say I'm good?"

Suddenly Kostokis's own memories flashed into his mind.

He recalled taking a wailing crack baby out from a furnace in a burning tenement; he had given a teenage junkie a second chance by getting her into a drug rehab program instead of busting her; he had carried his former partner, Rita Gallagher, out of the line of fire after a gangbanger shot her in the back.

"But I've got flaws the same as anyone else."

"You may not always be fair and just," Stanley said. "But you're as fair and just as any man can be in this corrupt world."

Before Kostokis could protest any further, he fell back into the darkness.

Kostokis blinked several times as he emerged from the depths of Stanley's mind.

Wheezing, Stanley took the stone out of his jacket pocket and shoved it into Kostokis' hand. The detective cried out as it glowed hot and burned his flesh. He dropped the rock and clutched his hand.

Power rushed into his mind like a tidal flood.

61

"Make them all confess," Stanley said, his voice pained.

"Wait," Kostokis said.

Stanley made a choking sound and collapsed in the snow.

"Help!" Kostokis said.

A few people came running as Kostokis knelt and performed CPR on Stanley despite the bum's stink and the pain in his hand.

But it was too late.

Afterwards, he stepped back from the crowd, picked up the now inert stone and stumbled away. As he fled, he took a handkerchief from his pocket and wrapped it around his burnt hand.

The stone held such power, Kostokis thought. Where was it from, though? And was it good or evil or nei-ther?

He didn't know and couldn't say.

Kostokis stopped at a bridge near the park's lake and looked at the stone.

What do I do? Kostokis thought. I could make so many others confess, but what would it do to the world?

Hell, I could bend them all to my will and make them do even more than confess.

But no, it would be wrong to take advantage of people as Stanley had.

Kostokis reached back to hurl the stone. At the last moment, though, he stopped.

What if I could do some good, though? Kostokis thought. Perhaps I shouldn't be so hasty.

After a moment's hesitation, Kostokis pocketed the rock and walked away.

About The Author

Fredrick Obermeyer enjoys writing science-fiction, fantasy, horror, and crime stories. He has had work published in NFG, Electric Spectrum, Newmyths, Perihelion SF, Acidic Fiction, the Destination: Future anthology, and other markets.

Now Available In Trade and Electronic Editions from Most Retailers

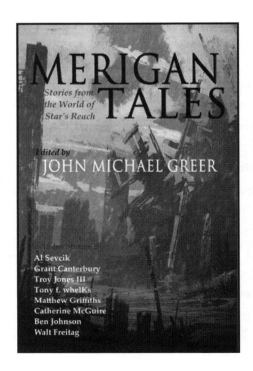

IN MAGIC LANDS

BY LAWRENCE BUENTELLO

I'm an old man now, but when I was a boy my family lived next door to Jay Long and his mother and father. They were a secretive family, but because people at the time valued privacy more than they do today, their neighbors never pried into the nature of their secrets, but respected their right to live their lives in the way they preferred, as long as they obeyed common standards of decency. So the mother and the father, whose names I never committed to memory, practiced a polytheistic religion my parents frowned upon but tolerated in their mistaken belief in the innocuousness of foreign primitivism. Since the Longs rarely spoke of their religion or decorated their house with icons illustrating it, no one ever threatened them or tried to remove them from the neighborhood. They eventually moved on their own, perhaps because the memory of their son became too painful and they wished to begin their lives anew, without constant reminders of his

death. I don't know what became of them. But they never mattered to me—only their son.

Jay and I were both seven years old when he told me of the Magic Lands.

Our backyards adjoined, separated by an old wood fence with numerous broken slats, and since neither of us had siblings, we traded turns slipping through the fence to play in the other's yard. Neither his parents nor mine had much money, which meant that whatever amusement we invented on hot summer days, or cold winter days, arose from the natural Texas surroundings and our youthful imaginations. *My* imagination contributed adventures in space, military expeditions into the African desert or across the waters of the Rhine, or the exploits of cavalry soldiers as they fought to conquer the Old West, invigorated by what I read in comic books or the newspaper my father discarded every morning. During these play sessions the objectives were predictable: conquer the planet Mars, survive an attack of German soldiers, or save the fort from marauding Apaches.

But Jay conjured very different scenarios, and if I had been a little more mature, or a little more intelligent, I might have seen the genius behind the beautiful imaginary constructs he described. Years later, with the assistance of my parents' recollections, I deduced that Jay and his parents were Polynesian, or Pacific Islanders, but I never knew the specifics of their heritage; I simply wasn't paying enough attention to rescue any relevant clues regarding their origins. As I said, the desire to respect Jay's family's privacy prevented anyone from knowing too much about them. They never volunteered the information. But they must have kept their connection to the supernatural world in their daily rituals, because Jay conducted his life through its influence. I was witness to this connection, and I believe in the truth of my experience. I remember his dark eyes, his thick, black hair, and the enigmatic smile that shouldn't have belonged to an ordinary little boy, a smile holding many secrets. Perhaps too many for a boy his age.

Once we were through dramatizing the stereotypes of the American West, Jay would guide us through magnificent jungles populated by singing monkeys and fabulously colored birds whose bright red, green, and gold tails spread out beneath them like the hems of elegant gowns. We passed beneath the splashing foam of waterfalls taller than skyscrapers, paddled in canoes across brilliant blue mountain lakes, and hacked our way through lush undergrowth with the assistance of machetes that were really only branches fallen from the oak tree in my yard. Once we had forged our way through the natural barriers, Jay would bring us into ancient stone cities built before the Sumerians pressed marks into clay tablets. These cities were inhabited only by the ghosts of the people who once occupied their structures, people who were wise and noble, who had ceased warring with one another in order to create lovely works of art in stone, majestic statues adorning the great halls of knowledge, bas-reliefs of animals and beasts, and fountains pouring pure streams of water into marble ponds full of red and white carp and other exotic fish.

I say this now, because I believe it to be true—as we wandered through the Magic Lands, as Jay described them in a quiet, musical voice full of the confidence of someone who *knows* his descriptions to be genuine, I began to see the world he narrated actually materializing around us.

This didn't happen immediately; for a while I saw nothing but the patches of grass and islands of dirt of either yard, and the sticks we carried, as we stomped from one corner of the fence to another, were only sticks. The jungle he so beautifully described was completely invisible. But slowly, as the days passed and our adventures continued, I began to see things manifest in the sunlight that bore no resemblance to a house or fence or grass, at first as if small mirages were appearing before my eyes, but the weather wasn't warm enough yet for the heat to radiate visibly from the ground. No, these visions floated before me as if projected onto the air, wispy, then becoming more tangible, the trees of the jungle, the vast tapestry of vines, and, more startlingly, the shapes of wild monkeys and jungle cats slipping through the foliage.

These wild sights swam before us superimposed on the ordinary sights of a suburban landscape, and at first I was afraid—but I was only a boy, and the young have a marvelous capacity to accept new perceptions of the world, no matter how strange. My fear dwindled, and my excitement grew with every new adventure into the jungles and ancient cities Jay wrought from his extraordinary imagination. We actually traveled through these jungles, which came to supplant every sense of the houses and the backyards with their own reality, the Texas birdsongs were drowned out by the howls of the monkeys screeching in the jungle canopy, the gentle rustling of the breeze through leaves was absorbed into the bellicose roar of the waterfalls we passed. I could feel the stone escarpments of the cities we explored against my palms; Jay would lead, and I would follow, and every day the Magic Lands became more real than the common life that waited for us at journey's end.

I often told my parents about our adventures, waving my arms at the dinner table as I tried my best to illustrate the treasure rooms we had visited, the enchanted mirrors we viewed, the pools of murky water inhabited by silent faces peering from the depths—but I didn't have Jay's verbal talent, and they only shook their heads and wondered between themselves if I should be spending so much time with the child of heathens. Eventually I learned not to relate our adventures—they were too exciting to abandon, and even though I was still a child intimidated by religious mores, I wouldn't give up our explorations just to avoid the hellfire of Western beliefs.

There *is* real magic in the world— I've seen it, experienced it myself, in the best empirical fashion. Or, at least, I did as a child.

The summer Jay died was very hot. Back in those days, a great many homes didn't possess air-conditioning, or, if they did, it was confined to one or two rooms and produced by window units. Neither my house nor Jay's possessed even a window unit, and so every summer proved to be a trial by sweat and sleepless nights. My parents meant well when they bought a small plastic swimming pool for me to cool myself during those endless summer days. It held about a foot or so of water, and the first day I sat in it beneath the ruthless midday sun I sank down until the water lapped coolly at my chin. I wished I could have summoned a more exotic imaginary experience to accompany prosaic reality, but the best I could do was to close my eyes and imagine I was floating in one of the crystal pools of the ancient cities. But when I opened my eyes the summer sun still blazed above me, and I was still in my own backyard in a plastic swimming pool.

Inevitably, Jay squeezed through the space left by a missing fence board and found me lounging in the water. He laughed wildly as he peeled off his shirt and pants and climbed in—I was happy to share the coolness of the pool with him, and expected nothing more hazardous than having water splashed in my face. After a moment, though, Jay began describing another adventure, and I listened raptly, expecting to embark on a new exciting journey. Adam, he said, we're no longer in a swimming pool in Texas. We're in a raft on the ocean trying to find the Mysterious Island of the Fathers. The waves are tossing us like dolls in a basket, the skies are dark with storm clouds booming their old voices above us—

Suddenly, as if I'd been struck across the eyes by a vicious gale, the yard blurred before me, but then quickly rematerialized into a world much more dangerous than my own.

We were seated in a raft in the middle of the ocean, rising and falling with the swells; the sky above was torn into ribbons of blackness and dazzling white lightning bolts, as cold rain dropped onto us like darts and the wind screamed maniacally in our ears. The storm and the sea roiled into blinding sheets of water that beat on us brutally; I could barely see Jay at the front of the raft, a shadow glazed by lightning-fused droplets. I clung to the sides of the raft and cried out, certain I would be flung into the ocean and lost. But *would* I be lost? Where would I go? Would I sink to the bottom of the sea? For me, this was not a fun adventure, this was terrifying, and I didn't care where the Island of the Fathers was, or why it was so mysterious. I wanted to be back home under the summer sun, safe in my own backyard. I closed my eyes against the stinging rain and shouted at Jay repeatedly, please, please take us back! Take us back!

He did. In an instant the storm vanished, the heaving motion of the raft settled into stillness, and I found myself sitting in the plastic pool with Jay staring at me as if I'd lost my mind. It was only an adventure, he'd said, moving his hands in and out of the water. Why did you get so scared?

I *had* been scared—I'd been terrified, because I knew it had been real. Wherever we had gone, into whatever reality his mind had taken us, I knew it wasn't playtime any longer. I stared at him and suddenly didn't want to be his friend. I wanted to be safe in my own world, not a magic world, no matter how beautiful.

You go, I said as I stood in the water and then stepped out of the pool. I wish I hadn't said this. I wish I had said something else, but I did say it. You go by yourself if you want to, I don't want to go. Go by yourself.

I *will*, he said, the sunlight shining in his dark eyes, his smile bearing something other than bravery. Perhaps he wanted to prove to me that our latest adventure hadn't been treacherous at all—perhaps he truly believed we hadn't been in any danger—

I ran inside my house. I ran without looking back, leaving Jay sitting alone in the small plastic swimming pool in shallow water.

I stayed in my bedroom the rest of the day, sitting among the shoes in my closet as I read the same comic book over and over again, until the screaming began, risen from Jay's mother's throat. *My* mother had found Jay in the pool, drowned in a foot of water. The police came, and I sat by the window in my room saying nothing, thinking nothing, letting reality take its course. No one understood how a seven year old boy could drown in such a small pool of water. It was a tragic accident, a freak event. Perhaps he'd had a seizure in the sun—but a seizure hadn't ended Jay's life.

All this happened many years ago, and now I'm an old man, having lived a long and tedious life absent of enchantment. When I die, I will die with the knowledge that I left that place behind, along with my friend, and that he might have survived, or I might have died, too, had I traveled with him to one of the lethal places of the Magic Lands.

About The Author

Lawrence Buentello has published over 100 short stories. He enjoys writing in a wide variety of genres, including science fiction, fantasy, and horror. Aside from fiction, he writes poetry and the occasional essay. Buentello also has over 25 years of experience working in academic libraries, which has kept him as close to the written word as possible. He lives in San Antonio, Texas.

BREATHERS

BY WENDY NIKEL

Henry Bean had a miserable retirement—all six months, two weeks, one day, and six hours of it—until the world went wrong and the man behind all the controls of the New South Central Railroad paid him a visit.

"Just one more run, Henry."

"I'm retired now, you know." Henry gestured to the crossword puzzle book on his armchair. Isn't that what retired folks did? Never mind that Henry had already solved all the puzzles at least four times. As long as he used a pencil, he could erase the answers and fill them in again another day.

"Yes. I was at the party, remember? I presented you with that fob watch."

"I had that stroke, you know." Henry rested his elbow on his oxygen respirator. The blasted thing had been his constant companion since the day they'd found him doubled over in the observation car and made an unscheduled stop to rush him to a hospital. In New Jersey, of all places.

He'd hated that the stroke made the train late for its arrival in Chicago. Doubly hated that it had forced him into retirement. Triply hated that because the thing cost so much, he wasn't even able to retire someplace warm and sunny with a view of the sea. Though that was partially the fault of the Plague, too. His retirement really couldn't have come at a worse time.

"We can make accommodations," the railroad man said. "You can bring your oxygen tanks, and we'll have someone there to help you up and down the steps. We're offering triple pay for anyone who volunteers."

"How come none of the other conductors are jumping on the opportunity? How come you have to come bothering a poor old man like me?"

The pause stretched on so long that Henry wondered if the Plague had begun to effect folks' hearing as well. No, that wasn't it. If the railroad president had the Plague, Henry would've known. He wouldn't still be standing in his doorway, wringing his hands like an altar boy at confession.

"This is a one-way trip, Henry."

Henry reached into the pocket of his bath robe and fiddled with the fob watch. They'd engraved it with an image of a shark, knowing that he'd always wanted to see one in person but now wouldn't have a chance to. "Destination?"

"St. Louis. Further, if you can make it. In case you hadn't noticed, a lot has changed since you retired. I've hardly got enough employees left to keep the train running as it is. Too busy worried about their own families. Most have already headed west. I figured you might want to leave the city, too."

Henry stared at the cardboard covering his window. A single pinprick of light shone through, creating a thin beam that stretched across to the opposite wall. Since the electricity had gone out, he'd spent days watching that line move across the room. Before that, he'd at least had his crosswords and *Wheel of Fortune* and the news (when he couldn't find the remote control fast enough to change the channel). Every day, the newscasters would try to keep the panic from their voices as they recounted the eerie green clouds carrying the Plague, the citywide crime and looting and folks crying in the streets. Every day, they failed to reassure him.

He'd been relieved when the power went out, so he could pretend everything was normal again. Or at least as normal as it could be in a pitch-dark world where folks closed themselves up indoors after sunset. The silence was sometimes deafening.

Henry's thoughts had wandered so far that he was surprised to see the railroad man still standing there, waiting for an answer.

"So... will you do it?"

"Yeah. I'll do it."

Though he'd given himself an extra hour to get down to the station, there wasn't a taxi to be found, so Henry shuffled to the bus stop. The old beast was in pretty bad shape, with broken windows and graffiti on the sides, but at least it ran. That was more than could be said for most vehicles around here anymore.

Henry hobbled slowly up the steps, much to the chagrin of the heavyset driver and his load of sweaty, stinking passengers. Henry discreetly sniffed his own clothes, hoping that the cologne he'd sprayed would mask the fact that he hadn't had a decent bath in weeks. Once onboard, there wasn't a single passenger who would share their seat with a feeble old man, regardless of what he smelled like. They simply sat there, their bags spread out across both seats, trying not to meet his eye.

"Is this seat taken, ma'am?" he asked politely. The woman muttered "sorry," her voice muffled by the Plague mask covering her face.

Henry recounted what the somber-faced newscasters had said—that the specialized masks, which now cost thousands of dollars apiece, would only give very limited protection from the Plague. If there were enough Breathers around, particularly in a small space like this, the germs would eventually find their way through the filter. The woman glared at him, and Henry shuffled past.

This strange, suspicious world would take some getting used to.

By the time the bus pulled into the train station, Henry's left leg was stiff from standing and his shoulders ached from carrying his respirator. As promised, the engineer had come down to greet him and to help him mount the steps.

"Appreciate your service today, sir." The engineer looked young. Far too young to be in charge of a whole train. Either Henry was getting too old to accurately estimate others' ages, or the railroad had been scraping the bottom of the barrel to staff this trip.

Of course they had been, he realized. They'd asked *him*, hadn't they?

"You're taking us to St. Louis, then?"

"Yes, sir." The boy looked down the line of cars, his brow furrowed in concern. "If we make it."

"Why wouldn't we?"

The boy's eyes met his. "They really didn't tell you much about this trip, did they? Looks like I'm going to have to fill you in."

The train rumbled down the tracks. The passengers seated on the left-hand side could—if they were the sentimental type—peer out their windows at the shrunken skyline of their once-beloved city. This would be their last opportunity, so many of them chose to lean forward in their seats and crane their necks to catch the final glimpse of the life they were leaving behind.

The passengers on the right-hand side conspicuously avoided their windows. In one seat, a mother even used her jacket to block the view from her curious offspring. Their eyes each held the same expression: a mix of horror and apprehension, the same expression Henry had seen on the faces of every TV newscaster since this whole thing began.

Henry wished he could change the channel.

After punching tickets and making sure everyone was settled in, Henry leaned against the wall at the front of the train car, fiddling with the airflow on his respirator, trying to suppress his own anxiety for the sake of his passengers.

It hardly seemed proper to wish these poor folks a pleasant trip, nor did it seem appropriate to comment on the weather, seeing as it was those swirl-

71

ing, green-tinged clouds that brought the poisoned rain that got them into this mess in the first place. He frowned at the right-hand windows and the greenish glow they cast over the passengers.

What on God's green earth had he gotten himself into?

In the third row, a young couple sat with their fingers intertwined. The man clutched his cellular phone in one hand like a ragged security blanket. He pressed the 'on' button with his thumb—a nervous habit—but of course nothing happened. How long had it been since it had had electricity running through it? It'd been weeks since Henry's apartment had been lit up, but then again, some of these rich folks probably had backup generators that ran for a while. When the woman saw him looking, she reached over and gently took the phone from her husband, sadly meeting his eye as she placed it in his breast pocket. She held both his hands in hers.

In the sixth row, a mother held a fussy toddler, bobbing up and down a bit to soothe his cries. The boy clawed at the Plague mask on his face, but his mother gently removed his hands, not allowing him to tear it away.

"Excuse me, sir," she said as Henry hobbled down the aisle, "How long will it take to get out West?"

Henry scratched his chin. "Well, if all goes well"—he didn't want to mention the possibilities the engineer had warned him of: ambush, outbreak, tracks made impassible by lack of maintenance or blockades—"we should arrive in St. Louis in five hours."

"And it'll be safe there?"

"Well, from what I understand, weather systems tend to move west to east," he said, quoting what he had heard from the TV newscasters. "So once we are outside the bio-hazard radius"—he didn't know if that was the technical term, but it sounded intelligent—"then the incoming western weather systems should push the chemicals eastward, over the Atlantic."

The mother let out a sigh of relief, as if the distribution of hazardous biological chemicals over one of the world's largest bodies of water was a small thing, hardly worth caring about since she and her child would be safe. Well, relatively safe. As safe as one could get in this crazy world-gone-wrong.

"What's the boy's name?"

"Timothy." She stroked the child's hair. He arched his back against her, trying to break free of her grasp so that he could tug at the mask again. His eyes were puffy and red from crying, his hair sticky from sweat.

Henry's fingers—stiff and arthritic—fumbled with his fob watch, trying to undo the clasp. "Here. Why don't you play with this for a bit, little tyke?

Something to keep your mind off that itchy mask, huh? Look, I have one, too."

He reached behind him to the oxygen tank and placed the plastic mask over his nose and mouth. "I like to pretend I'm snorkeling. Have you ever seen pictures of folks snorkeling underwater? They dive way down under the surface and search for fish and coral and sharks. Like that guy on my watch. He's a hammerhead."

The boy's eyes widened at the mention of sharks. He peered at the watch in his hands.

"You be careful with that, Timothy. It must be very important to the conductor, and you wouldn't want to break it."

"Don't worry," Henry said. "I don't have much use for it nowadays, now that—"

Now that what? Now that there were no trains to keep on schedule? Now that society had collapsed?

"Thank you," the woman said, obviously grasping his meaning.

"I'll be back to check on you folks later."

Henry continued to make his way down the aisle, stopping here and there to offer folks a bottled water or bag of stale peanuts, and pausing even more often to catch his breath. They were out of soda pop and chocolate chip cookies and the other goodies that his trains usually carried, but the folks didn't seem to mind. They accepted his

gifts with grateful half-smiles and whispered 'thank you's that Henry had to strain his old ears to hear.

They were much calmer and more grateful than the folks on the bus, probably because these folks knew they were leaving, that in a few short hours the worst would be behind them. They were the lucky ones.

Way in the back, an old man snored, his white-whiskered chin pointed skyward.

"Well at least someone's able to get some rest." Henry chuckled and reached up to the storage rack to find a blanket to throw over him. Pinching the corners, he snapped it open and lowered it gently over the man's body. The man continued snoring.

No.

It wasn't a snore.

Oh, no. Not now. Not today.

Henry automatically reached for the oxygen mask on his respirator and pressed it over his face, breathing in deeply as he tried to still his racing heart. Was he having another stroke? Or just a panic attack?

Henry glanced down the aisle at all of the people sitting, unsuspecting, in their seats. His eyes teared up. He wished he hadn't gotten so close, hadn't seen for sure that those weren't snores coming from the old man's lips. If only he hadn't noticed... No. That would have made it worse. He knew what he had to do.

He pulled his mask from his face.

"Ladies and gentlemen," he said loudly. "Please remain calm. There's been a Breather identified in our car."

Pandemonium.

Folks rushed to the exits, to barricade themselves in the next car, not willing to admit that they had been breathing the same air as the infected man since the train rolled out of the station nearly an hour ago. It was too late for them, and they knew it. Soon they'd be gasping for breath as well, blacking out, turning into Breathers themselves. Henry knew it, too. He pressed the emergency button on the back door and radioed the engineer on his battery-operated walkie-talkie, following the procedures that had been described to him.

"We got a Breather." His voice cracked. "Car 3. Unhook us."

The passengers pounded on the doorway to the next car, but as Henry looked out the window, all he could see was the railroad worker jumping out of the car and going to work at severing the cables that tied their car to the one ahead of it. The uninfected cars behind them would have to be pulled back to the nearest switch and take a different line out west. It was a calculated risk one took when riding the train. This is why the railroad man couldn't get any other conductors. This is why he'd offered such a high price for this trip. He'd known there was a

chance that something like this might happen.

Desperately, men pried at the windows, tugging on them until their fingernails broke and bled. The frames had been welded shut in case of a situation like this. Containment was the only thing to keep the poison from spreading, to keep these folks—now carriers—from spreading the Plague even farther.

The couple in the third row still clutched one another's hands. Timothy's mother sobbed, her head bent protectively over her child. The Breather rasped louder and louder, drowning out the gradually-slowing rattle of the train wheels. By this point, they all knew they were done for. If you're close enough to a Breather to hear its rasping, then it's too late.

Unless...

"Hey! That kid has a mask!" someone shouted. A few men and women rushed forward, but Henry blocked their path, his shoulders squared.

"Leave the boy alone," he said. "It's too late for you, and you know it."

As if on cue, one of the women collapsed, clutching the edges of the seats as a harsh, grating rasping emitted from her mouth. The others backed away, leaving her lying in the middle of the aisle alone.

One by one, the passengers fell.

Henry looked down at Timothy, whose eyes were wide and frightened over his Plague mask. It wouldn't protect him for long, not trapped in here with a carload of Breathers all exhaling their poisoned fumes. But there was something Henry could do.

He reached down and started the oxygen flowing on his respirator. His own breath was already ragged, though he didn't know if it was the effects of the stroke or the Plague. It didn't matter. Either way, he wasn't going to survive this. Either way, there was only one person here who might.

"Timothy, would you like to be a snorkeler? Would you like to pretend you're diving down to see the fishies?"

At first, Timothy shook his head, but his mother—now fighting for breath—whispered in his ear, and slowly, he nodded.

"Okay, Timothy," Henry said. "I need you to pretend that this whole train car is the ocean. Don't breathe in until you've got your snorkeling mask on, okay? The train men will come to get the other cars, and when they do, you wave to them and let them know you're in here, all right? They'll get you out, and when they do, you can take the mask off, but as long as you're on the train, you keep it on, all right? Are you ready?"

Henry gently removed the Plague mask, and before two seconds had passed, he had the oxygen mask pressed over the boy's face. It wasn't a perfect fit; the mask was designed for an old man, after all, but it might be able to provide him the protection he needed until rescue arrived.

"Do you see the fish, Timothy? Look, they're swimming over your head."

The rasping grew around them. Henry's lungs burned.

"There's an octopus hiding in that coral. And see the little sea stars, with the tiny suction cups on their legs?"

One by one, the people stilled. Soon, the only movement was Timothy's tiny fingers snapping the watch open and shut and the barely perceptible movement of Henry's lips.

"The ocean's so beautiful, Timothy, isn't it?"

Then he too, became still.

About The Author

Wendy Nikel enjoys a quiet life near Utah's Wasatch Mountains. She has a degree in elementary education, a fondness for road trips, and a terrible habit of forgetting where she's left her cup of tea. Her short fiction has been published by Fantastic Stories of the Imagination, Daily Science Fiction, Nature: Futures, and various other anthologies and e-zines. For more info, visit wendynikel.com.

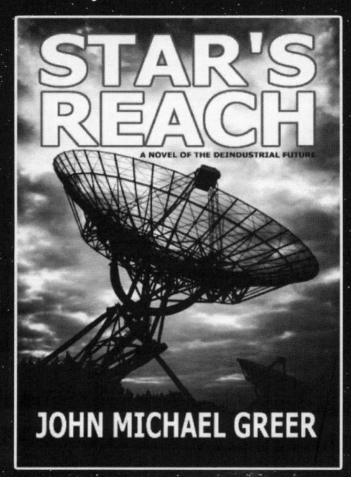

ENCOUNTER AT DURHEIM CROSSROADS

BY CHET GOTTFRIED

Derrick whipped off his helmet, threw it to the ground, and glared at his broadsword.

"You miserable twisted piece of rust. You'd bounce off a wad of butter. I'd prefer a willow rod to the likes of you."

He ignored the beauty of the dappled sunlight over the Durheim crossroads and took a huge breath.

"Why do all my strokes hit on the flat? Are you a sword at all? If a name means anything, you're a disgrace to the entire history of swordsmanship. From the first sword made down to the present, they're laughing at you. I'm laughing at you! Has anyone ever heard of a *real* weapon being called 'Elderberry'? Ha! Your name is ridiculous. You're ridiculous. Pathetic! I swear: I'll pay a blacksmith to hammer you into a doorstop. Better yet, I'll throw you into the first river or lake." Derrick shook his sword. "How do you like that?" he roared, shaking the nearby trees.

After a brief silence, Elderberry said, "Pull the other one."

Derrick's massive shoulders slumped. Years of being a warrior. Continually practicing to hone the skills necessary to enhance his reputation. And for what? To be insulted by his own sword. Life wasn't fair.

"That's another thing I hate about you. You've no respect."

"What does respect have to do with it?" Elderberry asked. "You shouldn't have insulted old man Nayshank. Any fool should have known better, especially someone who goes around and proclaims himself to be the top warrior in the land. Look at you! All muscles and no brains. No one else would alienate as nasty a wizard as you could hope not to meet. And why did you do it? Over a poem. Yeah, you're a class act."

"The rhyme was off," Derrick said.

"It comes down to the same thing: You're responsible for your own mess, so stop whining."

Derrick inhaled deeply and screamed his war cry. Branches throughout the grove shattered, a maple tree crashed on its side, and three crows dropped dead from the sky.

"I don't whine. I do what heroes do everywhere: boast, complain, or curse, to suit the occasion."

"Whatever."

He sighed. "So what's my count?"

Elderberry cleared its imaginary throat. "Thus far, to fulfill your geas, you've bagged twelve thieves and six warriors."

"Is that all? I've been at it for two months. Surely I must have wiped out more?" A thought leaped into Derrick's consciousness. "Hey! I've just finished subduing my seventh warrior."

Derrick's arm moved involuntarily as Elderberry took over control in order to point.

"You mean the guy who's standing over there?"

He looked, and sure enough, three yards away stood a huge warrior who was watching Derrick.

"What the . . . ? I thought you surrendered. I distinctly remember your yelling, 'stop,' and—"

At that precise moment recognition flared, and Derrick knew the warrior opposite him.

"Lord Gautrek!"

Gautrek wasn't a noble by either birth or grant, but his nickname came about from his extraordinarily good manners. While eviscerating an opponent, he'd say, "Excuse me," and his legend extended to his using a table napkin correctly. Gautrek dressed like a noble too and wore the latest accessories. His helmet had a silk fringe and a griffin flight feather.

"Well met, Derrick the Mighty! Tell me, is it true you tore a hole through King Jacoby's castle?"

Fancy Gautrek hearing of his exploits! Derrick grinned broadly and nodded.

The two warriors rushed at each other and embraced in a bear hug along with much slapping and shouting. They laughed long and hard at the chance encounter of two legendary heroes.

Letting go and stepping back, Derrick apologized for their initial combat. "I lose all control because of the spell old Nayshank put on me. I would have never begun our duel if not for Elderberry, one of wizard Nayshank's jokes."

"Tell me about it." Gautrek angrily shook his sword. "Meet Fleabane, who would give your Elderberry a distinct challenge in the category of worst sword in creation."

"You don't mean wizard Nayshank got you too?"

"The same."

Derrick tsked in sympathy. "Then you can't use your right hand except to hold your sword while you're awake, which makes eating and drinking awkward and annoying. And try to have a wench understand why you're holding the sword while in bed. You know, there ought to be a law about wizards. Imagine entrapping the two of us. Together we'd be an army capable of subduing anyone or anything we wanted. So look what happens. We're stuck cleaning the countryside. By the way, how did you rile Nayshank?"

"I rearranged one of his poems into a ditty, which became more popular than anything he ever penned. And so here I am. I have to slay or vanquish forty thieves, or twenty-five warriors, or five trolls, or two dragons, or one elf king before I can throw away Fleabane."

"What a bummer. It's not as if you meet any dragons these days. And elf kings? Forget it. They're as common as hair on an egg—unless you want to spend the rest of your life on the northern steppes. Wait a mo. Did you say 'twenty-five warriors'? Nayshank hit me for thirty."

Gautrek shrugged. "What do you expect from an angry wizard? Consistency? Fairness? Would he have loaded us with these ridiculous weapons if he had any sense of decency? What bothers me the most is that Nayshank has isolated the totals: forty thieves *or* twenty-five warriors. A simple ratio shows eight thieves equals five warriors in his scheme."

Derrick kicked a pebble. "I was never good at math."

"Our swords do the counting for us. It's about the only thing they're good for."

"True enough," Elderberry said, "but Nayshank isn't what you'd call a mathematician either. He prefers simplicity: give him straight sums. If you want to see a wizard sweat, ask him about trigonometry. You have to face it. When you hit one of your totals, you'll be free, so you might as well start swinging at each other again."

Derrick and Gautrek exchanged glances and then each grinned.

"You've got to be kidding," Derrick said, "unless my defeating Gautrek or him defeating me counts more than a single fighter. We're each worth a dozen other fighters."

"Absolutely," Gautrek said. "And a dozen is a modest number, considering skill and reputation."

"Sorry," Fleabane said, "Nayshank didn't factor reputation or skill into his requirements. A fighter is a fighter."

"That finishes it." Gautrek asked Derrick, "What do you say about heading to the Vargas River? I heard there are a few trolls mucking about. Or we could go to Wythburn and clean up the town. It has a number of thieves."

Derrick nodded. "Excellent plans. I like the idea of teaming up. We'll get them coming and going. No one will escape." He grinned happily. "Lucky you stopped our senseless combat when you did. I might have done you serious damage."

Gautrek took a step backward. "I'd never ask anyone to stop in the middle of a brawl."

"I clearly heard you shouting 'stop.' No doubts about it."

Gautrek slapped his forehead. "That wasn't me. That was my sword Fleabane, who's always doing daft things."

"Ha!" Fleabane said. "It's easy to criticize, but I'm not so daft as to turn a wizard's poem into a limerick."

"I composed a ditty, not a limerick. If you fail to understand the difference, you'll remain a third-rate magic sword all your life." Gautrek told Derrick, "It's like you said: No respect."

Derrick agreed. "You can always tell a Nayshank weapon, but why did your sword ask us to stop?"

"Excuse me," Fleabane said. "I'm not deaf, and I'm right here. If you have any questions, you can address me directly. However, since you're a foolish mercenary at best, you don't have to repeat your inane question."

"Very wise," Elderberry said. "You've no idea what I have to put up with."

"The point is this: I yelled 'stop' because the fellow on the left (or your right) has been trying to catch your attention for the past half-hour. He has waved, coughed (politely), and smiled at the two of you. Honestly, esteemed warriors should pay attention to everything happening around them. Some folks call it a sixth sense, being battle aware. Otherwise, how would you know if an enemy is creeping up from behind and ready to skewer you in the back? It is beyond me how the two of you manage to stay alive as long as you have—I say this while noting the gray streaks in your hair."

Derrick stomped on the ground. "I don't have gray hair."

"Nothing a little hair dye couldn't cure," Elderberry said. "Combing now and again would be another bonus."

Whatever the state of his hair or its color, Derrick had to admit the cranky Fleabane was correct. They had company.

A slim man stood nearby and waved to them. The stranger wore an elegant silk shirt, silk pantaloons, and a bright green silk scarf. His well-decorated scabbard hung from an equally well-decorated sword belt. A thin silk band kept his blond hair neatly in place. He also wore a diadem which had a single but remarkably clear diamond. He had pointy ears.

Derrick's mouth fell open. "An elf?"

"An elf king," Gautrek said.

The stranger stepped closer and bowed slightly from the waist.

"You are correct. I'm King Nerianna, and I'm hoping one of you fine fellows would tell me which of these footpaths leads to Durheim."

The two warriors turned toward each other and each winked. They could taste freedom.

Nerianna said, "I seldom venture this far south, but I received an invitation from my friend Otis to take part in a poetry festival."

"Poetry festival?" Derrick asked.

"Yes, the Tenth Annual Durheim Arts Festival, although in this case the arts involve poetry, from epic verse to sonnets to free form. I expect one and all will have a rousing time. Perhaps once you've settled whatever you're trying to settle between yourselves, you will come along with me. As they say, the more the merrier."

"It's not that simple," Derrick said.

A frown crossed Nerianna's face. "Oh dear, I dislike complicated directions. I have a tendency to get lost, and I wouldn't want to miss the festival. I'm the guest of honor."

"The directions are simple," Derrick said, "but you're not going anywhere. Wizard Nayshank put a spell on me."

"Me too," Gautrek said.

"I am surprised," Nerianna said. "Otis Nayshank is such a friendly fellow and the one who made sure I would be the guest of honor at the festival."

The elf king annoyed Derrick. "How long have you been standing here? Haven't you paid any attention to what we've been talking about?"

"You mean eavesdrop?" Nerianna put his hand over his heart. "That's hardly the proper thing to do among strangers."

"Okay," Derrick said, "it's like this. Your friend the wizard's spell means I have to hold the dumbly named sword Elderberry until I kill forty thieves, thirty warriors, five trolls, two dragons, or an elf king."

"Same here," Gautrek said, "except I only have to kill twenty-five warriors and my dumbly named sword is Fleabane."

"And they talk," Derrick added. "You wouldn't believe how insulting a sword can be, especially one named Elderberry."

The elf king became very pale. "Did Nayshank's geas actually specify an 'elf king'?"

The grim expressions on both Derrick and Gautrek did not require any further answer.

"I find it hard to believe Otis Nayshank would invite me to a poetry festival in order to murder me."

"Are you sure there's a poetry festival?" Elderberry asked.

"Otis sent me a broadsheet listing all the details. Surely you don't think that it is all a part of a trap to ensure I'd be in the area?" No one answered, and Nerianna continued. "There is only one way to find out. I'll go to Durheim, and

81

if there isn't any festival, Otis will have much to answer for. My magic is nowhere as potent as his overall, but I can lay a hex to make him think twice before pulling any such fraud again."

Derrick edged over toward where he had thrown his helmet, picked it up and put it on. "Excuse me, King, but it doesn't matter whether there is or isn't a festival. In order to free myself from Nayshank's spell, you have to die. The facts may not be pleasant, but they are the facts."

Nerianna took a deep breath. "If so, would you mind telling me which path leads to Durheim? You won't have the opportunity of answering after I slay you."

Derrick wondered what chance the slight elf thought he had against two preeminent warriors. "You don't have to go there. You'll be dead. Accept it."

"Let's say I get lucky and win. Then there won't be anyone to tell me the way, and I have worked so hard on the poetry competition too. Devising a good rhyme for 'brachiopod' isn't easy."

"Brachiopod?"

"You see! I told you it was difficult. How many poets or fighters have heard of brachiopods? You haven't? . . . A brachiopod is like a clam, but whereas a clam has a bilateral symmetry along the horizontal plane, a brachiopod has its bilateral symmetry on the vertical plane."

Derrick and Gautrek exchanged glances. Was the elf king entirely sane? Might he be an imposter? Derrick said, "If you kill Gautrek and me, either of our swords will tell you the way to Durheim. They've a better sense of direction than we have."

The elf king shook his head. "That won't do at all. You see, your swords are not truly magical, inasmuch as their magic won't pass from generation to generation or from user to user. They're ordinary weapons under a curse. Both Elderberry and Fleabane are goblins, who doubtlessly upset Otis, and they're doing servitude."

"Goblins!" Gautrek said. "I should have guessed."

"As soon as you either die or complete your geas, the spirit will return to its own body, which is presently in a state of suspended animation."

"Huh?"

"Their bodies are asleep for the duration," Nerianna said. "Therefore, I cannot count on their being around after I dispatch you. Next, consider all the complaints the two of you have made regarding your swords. Do you think they'll behave any better while you duel with me? I assure you my own sword is of the highest quality. Would you like me to list its attributes?"

"You needn't bother," Derrick said. "The way I see it, Elderberry with me or Fleabane with Gautrek didn't have anything to lose if either I or Gautrek died early on. It all stops with you. They get their freedom, unless the first person to fight you wins, and the other guy is stuck." The thought immediately struck him that Gautrek might have the first turn. Gautrek's sword noticed the elf king first. Derrick bet the very thought was going through Gautrek's mind.

"Take the east path from here," Gautrek said. "It will take you straight to Durheim. The journey may take a couple of days, but you'll come across several pleasant inns along the way."

"Thank you," Nerianna said.

"What are you playing at, Gautrek?" Derrick demanded. "Why tell the elf anything?" Who ever said that jerk was a lord? What a laugh! The guy was a fraud with a few gimmicks. Take that griffin feather—an obvious fake.

Gautrek straightened and looked at Derrick. "I intend to duel the elf, so I wanted to get the information out of the way."

"First?" Derrick growled.

"Aye, first. Why not. I spotted him first."

"You did not," Derrick shouted. "Your sword saw him."

"What's the difference?"

Derrick couldn't see any difference, but the point was as good an introduction to a fight as any.

"Over my dead body," Derrick said.

Nerianna interrupted. "You're not going to fight again?"

"What's it to you?" Derrick snarled.

"You were already at it for a half-hour with no results, so why not try something else? I've a deck of cards. Why don't you draw to see who goes first?"

"I appreciate the gesture," Derrick said, "but warriors have only one way of settling an argument, which is by the sword, even if ours are reincarnated goblins."

"Not reincarnated," Elderberry grumbled. "Can't you keep anything straight?"

Derrick ignored his sword. "Only one thing, King: if you'll agree to stay until Gautrek and I settle our dispute."

"You might slay each other. It's such a waste."

"We have to," Gautrek said. "It's the only way to be rid of these cursed swords."

Nerianna waved his arms. "I yield."

Derrick and Gautrek looked at each other.

"Excuse me," they said.

"I yield, so that ends it. You don't have to fight."

Derrick tried dropping Elderberry but to no avail. Gautrek also remained stuck to Fleabane.

Derrick hated having to kill anyone who proved to be a decent sort. Nerianna wasn't making it easy, and Derrick anticipated having nightmares after chopping down the elf. He scratched his head.

"We appreciate your trying, but it isn't so simple. You have to be sincere about giving up."

"I am sincere," Nerianna shouted.

"Our swords don't believe you. Chalk up another score to settle with Nayshank."

Nerianna turned his back. "I don't have to watch you fight to the death."

Derrick and Gautrek squared off and began their duel. The woods rang with the vicious cuts they swung at each other. Soon, breathing rapidly, they both withdrew a little ways. Derrick prepared for a final all-out attack and ran screaming at Gautrek, who screamed and counterattacked.

Their swords met with a tremendous clang and shattered, sending thousands of steel shards into the sky.

Gautrek stared into the fragment cloud. "I see a rainbow."

"Look out," Derrick cried, "they're coming back!"

The splinters rained down while screaming, as if each one had a goblin inside. After a few seconds of standing frozen in place, with one metal splinter whizzing close to Derrick's eye, both warriors relaxed. Shards blanketed the ground around them, but they had avoided the fall.

"I thought I was a goner," Derrick admitted.

"Me too," Gautrek said.

A quarter of Elderberry was left in Derrick's hand. "Speak for yourthelf."

Fleabane had a mere three inches of blade beyond the hilt. "Yeth."

Then the two swords fell to the ground and were, thankfully, silent.

Derrick kicked the hilt away. "They don't make magic swords the way they used to."

"When I was a kid a geas could ruin you from the day you received it until the day you died miserably. Now . . ." Gautrek shrugged.

"I surrender," Nerianna said weakly.

The two warriors looked at him. The elf king lay on his back, pinned by sword fragments.

"So we actually fulfilled the wizard's spell." Derrick grinned. "Would you believe it?"

"I believe it," Nerianna said. "What do you say about releasing me?"

Derrick turned toward Gautrek. "Shouldn't he give us something in return, his being a king and all?"

Gautrek nodded. "I'd like that poem about the brachiopods. Signed of course."

About The Author

Chet Gottfried is an active member of SFWA, with stories in *Jim Baen's Universe*, *Aboriginal SF, and Isaac Asimov's SF*, along with a large variety of stories in small press and online publications. He is the author of several novels, including his most recent SF book, *Into the Horsebutt Nebula*. Chet lives with his wife Sue and three ex-feral cats in State College, Pennsylvania.

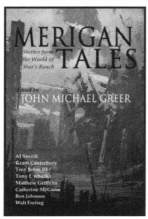

Now Available
from all your favorite booksellers
in trade paper and electronic editions

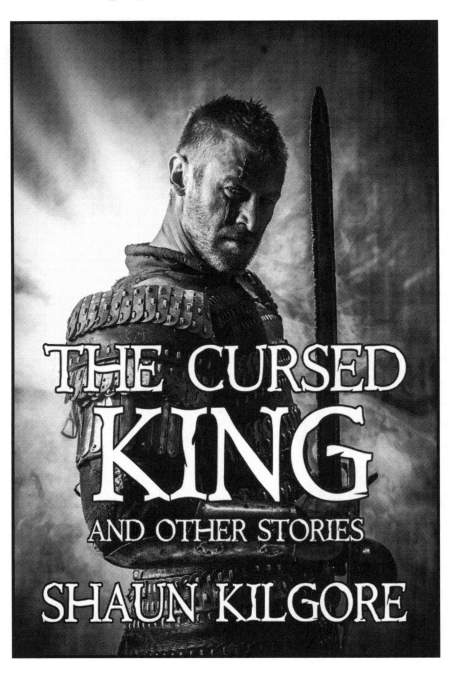

SPLOTCH

BY C.R. HODGES

Hildi Schreiber sat atop a streetlight, watching a couple of thirty-somethings make out on a park bench. When the man's hand disappeared under the woman's hospital scrubs, Hildi shimmied down. She contemplated a fly-through, guaranteed to seriously dampen their ardor. Instead, she scuffed her feet on the gravel path as she headed up one of the many open space trails that surrounded Boulder.

The gravel, however, refused to acknowledge her footprints.

She'd been sixteen for exactly five years, a difficult age under normal circumstances, and being dead hardly qualified as normal. The prospect of a twenty-first birthday party at a bar with giggling friends, downing shots and trying to figure out which guy to flirt with, was not to be hers. "I'm gonna be like a million-year-old virgin," she yelled at the trees. Which also denied her a response.

Being a ghost sucks.

Tucked under the boughs of an epic-sized blue spruce, the foot of a sleep-ing bag twisted violently. *Another couple getting it on.* But it was just a grizzly of an old dude, his beard a tangle of gray curls, umber eyes staring up blankly.

"You can't be dead," she said, taking a halfhearted kick through his knees as she trudged past. A rusted roach clip lay in the dirt. "I saw you move."

His head jerked up, eyes still blank. "Leavemealone."

Either he had some really potent weed that allowed him to see ghosts, or he was having one hell of a stoner dream. Probably back at Woodstock. Or Vietnam—a small American flag stuck out of his backpack. "Sorry, Bud," she said. There wasn't anything she could do, literally.

"Itsokaydontworry," he sighed, head settling back, blank eyes starward again.

Sleep tight.

When she circled back around to the knoll, heavy breathing and a few moans announced that the amorous pair was still at it. "Get a room," Hildi shouted, but not unexpectedly they completely ignored her.

But a dog did respond, a distant bark. *Good, bite the old letch's boner.* The barking continued, increasing. "Here, Doggie."

A small dog, off-white with patches of grayish brown, galloped up the path in slow motion. "Hey, you're not a Doggie, you're a Splotch." Talking to a dog beat talking to herself. Or to trees. she plopped down cross-legged on the leaf-covered ground. "Come here, Splotch."

The dog ran up to Hildi and stared her in the eye. Singular, for the dog had only one. Then Splotch licked her face.

Hildi swallowed. *Dogs can't see ghosts.*

Splotch was low slung like a basset hound but with the pointy ears of a shepherd. The one eye was nearly green, the other socket a mass of scar tissue. It—a she—gave Hildi another big lick, missing her cheek by a small amount but no matter.

"I'm down with that."

Splotch leaped up, wagged her tail and ran in circles around Hildi.

"Sure wish I spoke dog-ish," she said. "Woof, woofie woof."

The dog gave Hildi a *you're a crazy-ass ghost girl* look, head tilted.

Hildi pretended to pick up a stick and fling it toward the bench. "Fetch."

Head down, butt up, Splotch obeyed, legs moving in full gallop, straight toward the couple, the woman now kneeling in front of the man. Splotch barked joyously as she ran, but the woman didn't look up and the man was far too busy reciting *Oh fucks* like that was part of the rosary.

Splotch leaped as she reached the bench and passed through the woman's slumped shoulders. And the man too. He stood up, bare-assed, and grunted, "Be right back."

"Gotta gho pee mister?" Hildi yelled, laughing, as the man watered a dormant sapling. *Gho* was an inside joke, her self-anointed nickname that no one ever used. Unsurprisingly.

"Oh. Shit." She ran her hand through a thin layer of pine needles without disturbing a one. "Splotch be dead."

"*Rrrufff.*"

Perhaps the tenth such bark, Hildi admitted, as she slowly looked up. Splotch sat, tail wagging, a phantom stick in her translucent mouth.

"Poor, dead, good girl Splotch." Hildi wiped a phantom tear from her eye. "How did you come to be a ghost, puppy dog?"

Splotch headed back to the path. After thirty feet, she turned her head for a moment and then continued.

"Like I'm not going to follow a ghost dog on a mission. Let's gho."

Splotch wagged her tail and sped up.

As they pushed uphill into an urban forest, Hildi thought for a moment that Splotch was taking her to the homeless vet. But Splotch bounded past his spruce with just a quick yip. The woods thickened as they crossed a small ridge. When they emerged on a game track, Splotch barked.

No, a mountain bike track. A set of tread marks slashed across the path and into the brush.

Splotch barked again. Hildi dived into the thick brambles through which the bike had cut a one-time path, for once thankful for her ethereal state.

Two yards into the thicket the tracks disappeared off an embankment. Somewhere below, a creek gurgled, flush with spring runoff from the foothills. A young man sat on a tree stump, chin in hands, staring downward.

Hildi hmphed and said to herself, "Keep the training wheels on next time, duffus. C'mon, Splotch, let's gho." She turned around and headed back through the thicket.

"What are training wheels?" a lilted voice asked.

Hildi spun, jaw dangling. The young man was facing her, his left leg bent at an impossible angle, a gash across his dark forehead. "You're hurt."

"I think I died."

"Oh. Oh. I am sooo sorry. For saying mean things, for you dying, for... I'll shut up now."

"It is fine. I like your voice. Are you an angel?"

"Uh, I'm a ghost. Like you. It's not exactly heaven. No one to talk to."

"I like talking to you." His teeth almost glistened when he smiled. He was black, or had been, for as with Splotch, Hildi could see right through him. "Are you a ghost too?"

"Yup." He was kinda cute, gaping head wound notwithstanding. But ghosts could alter their appearance at will. She could teach him. "Would you like to gho somewhere and talk?"

He laughed. "Gho somewhere. That's funny."

He likes my jokes. "I know a nice jazz club where drinks don't cost anything, because, well, we can't drink. I'm Hildi." She pasted on a smile, flirtatious yet sincere. Hopefully.

"Mardan," he said softy, his voice fading along with his visage.

He hates my jokes. She wiped the smile. Probably looked cheesy. He's leaving. He doesn't like me.

A bark. Splotch. From down in the ravine. Hildi hurried down. At the bottom, a mangled bicycle lay on a boulder. Not a mountain bike at all, it was an antique single-speed bike like Grandma kept in her shed. A body lay next to the bike, motionless, one leg severely fractured below the knee. "Shit," Hildi hissed as she slid down the embankment. Splotch leaped past her and landed on all fours, stubby legs sticking through the spokes as if they were sunbeams.

Hildi kneeled beside the body. A black man, early twenties, sans helmet. Blood caked his close-cropped hair. "Quiet, Splotch. Er, sit," she said.

Splotch refused to sit but she did stop barking. Hildi put her ear to the man's chest. Nada. She took a deep breath of phantom air and lowered her head slightly through his rib cage, hovering over his heart. *Gross ick c'mon heart gross c'mon beat.*

Tha-themp. A single heartbeat. Infinitesimally faint, like she was on the moon rather than under the poor dude's skin.

Hildi counted. "One Mississippi. Two Mississippi..." At seven another paltry heartbeat. "He's alive, Splotch." *Barely.*

With a heart rate in single digits and fresh blood dribbling from his mangled leg. Hildi sat back on her haunches, her left hand petting Splotch. Except it wasn't Splotch, or at least not the ghost version. "Is this your body?" Hildi asked as she spun around. A carcass of a white dog with brownish patches, skull cracked on a rock, the rest of the body intact but lifeless. Already attracting a solitary fly despite the near freezing night. Hildi flailed at the fly. "Shoo."

The fly ignored her.

"What the fuck do I do now?" she asked a tamarisk.

"Elll..." the wind said as the junk trees rustled.

"Great, now I'm hearing things," she said. "Or are you talking to me, Splotch?"

The ghost dog tucked up under her arm and whimpered.

"Hel...ppp." Unless Splotch was also a ventriloquist, the voice was not coming from the dog. She looked down at the corpse, then thrust her ear back through his ribcage. At twenty Mississippis without a heartbeat a lilted voice, clearer now, said, "I believe I just died. Again."

A yip. Hildi looked up. The palest outline of a man stood over her, moonlight streaming through him like he was a gossamer curtain. "Mardan, is this your body?" she asked. Stupid question. "I'm sorry," she added, as he faded to nothing.

Splotch licked Mardan's fractured skull like he was made of peanut butter. His body suddenly convulsed. Hildi put his head back down on Mardan's chest. A heartbeat had returned, albeit irregular and faint. "Good girl, but we gotta find help."

"Don't you dare die," she called over her shoulder as she struggled up the embankment. "No one should have to be a ghost."

Hildi raced back toward the park, Splotch at her heels. "Maybe we can herd randy Andy and his bobblehead girlfriend down here."

"What's the rush, sweetie?" A coarse voice, not at all wind like. The grizzled vet was sitting up in his sleeping bag.

Gray hair, grayer beard. *Oh.* Bad night. "Are you a ghost too?"

"Nope." He tugged on his jowl, which reddened slightly. "Reckon I've seen enough ghosts in my day, however, to know what one looks like. You, for instance, and the mutt."

Hands on hips, Hildi stared. "Where the hell have you seen a ghost before?" People who could see ghosts were stupidly rare.

"Nam. War brings out ghosts like deer to a salt lick."

"You're stoned."

"Constantly. Don't matter. I still see you."

"Ohhh-kaaay. Look, Buddy, there's been an accident, down the bike trail. Can you like call an ambulance?"

"Ambulance," he said, head back, with a cackle. "Best I can do. Ain't got no phone." He struggled out of the sleeping bag, his jeans a mass of holes, pasty skin visible in a dozen places.

"Can you come with me, find someone with a phone, get them to make the call?"

The man stared.

"Please. The dude is dying."

"Don't reckon no one's going to let the likes of me borrow a phone, even if there is anyone around this late. But I was a medic, back in the day." A faint smile. "And oddly enough, my name is Bud." He slapped a VFW cap on his head and stuffed his sleeping bag into a canvas backpack. "Lead on, McDuff."

"This way. And it's Hildi. Or you can call me Gho."

Bud looked at her and shook his head ever so slightly. "Let's go, Hildi."

Then again, maybe he'd said, *let's gho*. Hildi smiled.

Bud set a glacial pace, and they had not gone a hundred yards when the couple from the park emerged from the trees, arm in arm, laughing. The woman's scrubs were on inside-out; the man was bare-chested under his jacket.

"Phone potential," Hildi said.

"Can you help us?" Bud asked. "There's been an accident."

The woman tittered, eyes slightly glazed. "Who's *us*? You and your bottle?"

Hopefully she wasn't a doctor. Or a nurse. Because in either case her next patient was toast.

"Naw, he's high, not drunk," the man said. "Reeks of some pretty good shit. You help us out, old man. Give us your stash and maybe I won't rearrange your face."

"There's an injured fellow down the ravine. We need your—"

The man lashed out with his foot but the kick was more form than *umph*. Bud grunted, grabbed the man's leg and yanked upward. The man flipped backward, landing with a loud thud on the pine-cone-strewn ground. "Loan me your phone, asshole," Bud said. "Please."

The woman opened her shoulder bag. Bud held out his hand, palm up. But she pulled out a canister of mace and sprayed him in the face.

"Moootherrrfuuuckerrr," Bud screamed, clawing at his eyes. The shirtless man struggled to his feet, paused, and then launched a round-house kick at Bud's gut. The kick connected and Bud fell screaming to the ground. The woman rummaged through Bud's jacket, pulling out a dime bag. "He's ghastly," she said, as she pocketed the stash and wiped her hand on her scrubs. "Disgusting."

"Bitch," Hildi yelled, inches from the woman's face, but the couple jogged off, laughing.

"Water," Bud croaked. "Wash... eyes..."

"Got a water bottle in here?" Hildi rummaged through his ancient backpack. Beside the sleeping bag, all he had was an empty hip flask, a two-week-old donut and a bong. *Figures.*

Splotch was barking now, facing the ridge. "Gotta be a creek down the other side. C'mon, Bud, follow me."

She took his hand, not at all sure if he could feel her. He stumbled blindly after her up the trail. At the ridgeline he slipped and tumbled down the embankment. He landed with a grunt on top of Splotch's corpse. Blood smeared his forehead like war paint. "Damn, damn, damn."

"It's not your blood, keep going. But you're gonna need a tetanus shot," Hildi said. Ghost Splotch stood, tail down, beside the young man's body. His head had turned, but he lay really still. And the ravine was dry.

"This way, sir." That windy voice again. A shadowy Mardan flickered in and out. "There is a rivulet over here."

Bud lunged forward, falling to his knees and crawling the last three yards. He thrust his face into the running water. "Ahhh," he said as he pulled his head out. "Another ghost?"

"I'm afraid so," Mardan said.

"How long have you been...?"

"Only a minute or two. This time. I seem to..." He faded slightly.

"Fading equals good. Can you do CPR, Bud?" Hildi asked.

"In my sleep." Bud struggled to his feet. "Although I ain't been certified in nigh on twenty years."

"Screw certs, bring him back."

"Please," the ghost said softly, squatting down beside Bud. More visible now.

Not a good sign. More ghost equaled more dead.

Bud set to work, three shoves on the chest and one breath into the Mardan's pale lips. His ghost grimaced.

"Hey, it's CPR, dude, it's not like he's kissing you," Hildi said.

"No, it is just, well, I felt that."

"Keep at it, Bud. If his spirit can feel you, he's not dead dead yet." *As if I really know jack about this.* "Don't you dare stop."

Bud tried three more chest compressions. Nothing. Arm held high, he slammed his fist down. The body jumped like it had been jolted with a few million volts, and Mardan's ghost vanished. A moment later, however, the ghost reappeared, gray face downcast. "I guess we can try that jazz club, now, Hildi." Mardan smiled wryly and reached out a translucent hand. "Maybe we can gho dancing afterward."

For a second Hildi smiled. "Love to, but not just yet. Bud, hit him harder!"

Bud belted the body. Nothing. Splotch yelped and jumped over Bud, landing on Mardan's lifeless face. Her gray tongue lapped out and gave Mardan a long, slow lick.

Mardan's ghost twitched.

"Not dead yet," Hildi yelled. "Bring him back to life, Bud. Like over in Vietnam."

"Yes ma'am." Bud pushed himself off the ground and threw his scrawny body into the chest compressions. "You'd have made a fine lieutenant."

"Damn right, but… hey, his ghost is gone." She squirmed in between Bud and the corpse and buried her ear inside Mardan's ribcage. "Bingo. Heartbeat."

Mardan lifted any doubts when he coughed once and then hurled.

"Get him water," Hildi yelled, but Bud was already sprinting toward the creek, empty hip flask in hand.

"Stay with me, Mardan," Hildi said, attempting to hold his hand but it slipped right through hers.

Using his teeth, Bud ripped Mardan's shirttail and wrapped it around his head wound. Mardan spat some of the water out and tried to prop himself up on one arm. "I think my leg is broken."

"Yup, among other things," Bud said. "Lie down and try not to move. What's your name, son?"

"It's Mardan, duh," Hildi said, but Bud ignored her.

"Mardan Nqarhwane. I am an exchange student from South Africa. Thank you."

"You're welcome," Hildi said. Except he hadn't looked her way once. A frown drooped down her face. *Oh.*

"What happened?" Bud asked, working on a splint.

"Biking to the university. My dog saw a coyote and panicked. I went into a skid." He raised his head and looked around. "Chaga? Where is my dog? Chaga!"

Bud laid a hand on Mardan's shoulder. "Stay where you are, son. Your dog is dead too."

Hildi rubbed Splotch's ear. Chaga's ear. "Tell him that Chaga saved his life." A much better name.

Bud nodded ever so slightly. "I think your dog saved your life. I... heard her barking."

"While I was unconscious, I dreamed that she was trying to save me." He paused. "There was a young woman too, with such beautiful eyes."

Beautiful. Hildi sighed.

"I thought perhaps I had died and she was an angel." Mardan sighed.

"It's a fucking sign!" Hildi said.

Bud slowly swiveled his head back and forth between Hildi and Mardan.

"Do you believe in angels?" Mardan was looking at Bud, but Hildi was sure he was talking to her.

"If you don't say yes, Bud, I'm going to haunt you to the end of your days," Hildi said.

"You need a doctor. Have you got a phone, Mardan?"

"Does not everyone in this country? Left rear pocket."

Bud fished it out.

"Do you need help with that?" Hildi asked, eyeing the smartphone.

Bud chuckled. "I said I didn't have a phone, not that I couldn't use one."

"Excuse me?" Mardan looked puzzled, but then his face blanched and he hurled.

"I talk to myself a lot, sorry. Hello, I need an ambulance... Eben Fine Park. GPS coordinates are..." He swiped the phone twice and then read off the longitude and latitude. "Victim's name is Mardan something or other. Exchange student... My name? Staff Sergeant Bud Coleman, US Army, Retired." He hung up. "On their way. They'll be taking you to Boulder Hospital, just up the street."

"Will you come with me?" Mardan asked.

"You bet," Bud said, squeezing his hand. "And yeah, I do believe in angels."

That's my cue. "C'mon, Chaga, let's gho spook a hospital," Hildi said. They walked up Broadway, into oncoming traffic. Cars zipped right through them. No one honked or swerved or even cast an askew glance. "If we can figure out which department Ms. Maceface works in, we'll teach her ghastly."

Chaga looked up with her good eye, tilted her head, and howled.

About The Author

C.R. Hodges writes all manner of speculative fiction, from ghost stories to urban fantasy to science fiction. Twenty of his short stories have been published in markets such as Cicada and Escape Pod, and he is a first prize winner of the 2016 Writer's Digest Popular Fiction Awards. When he is not writing or playing the euphonium, he runs a product design company in Colorado where he lives with his wife, dog, and no ghosts that he knows of. His online haunts include crhodges.wordpress.com and www.facebook.com/C.R.Hodges/Author.

HOLDING HANDS

BY ERIC NASH

"According to this, a Ruckus Mogunt held sway over the land between here and Digby Oak."

"Ruckus Mogunt? Who was he?" Richard asked, his hair and eyebrows wet from walking through an unexpected morning mist.

Anna pointed to the information plaque outside the long barrow. The cuff of her jacket slipping back to reveal the dots, dashes and solidus tattooed on the back of her thin right hand, which deciphered read, 'I am'.

"He was King of the Hill."

"Mmm, I think I'm going to be King of the Hill."

Climbing above the moisture-heavy air to the top of the mound, Richard was almost toppled by a couple of swallows swooping by him to dart through the open entrance of the barrow. Their high-pitched chatter had an urgency to it that continued even when he reached the brow to witness the sun rise.

Surveying the sea of farmland to where the earth's contours shaped the skyline brought him a wave of comprehension: despite never visiting here before, Richard knew this place. As his body turned to follow the horizon, he became dizzy from the sensation of familiarity. It wasn't that he recognized the three oaks that were dotted like sentries north-west, or the litter of standing stones north-east, or even the weaving road on which the occasional car glided. None of that meant anything to him because he imagined, no, remembered it being a forest, and it had been his home. That was absurd, of course: he had never been there before and there was no way he could know what this landscape had actually been like.

He was careful not to mention his deja-vu to Anna who, with her drawing pad on her lap, was perched on top of the large sarsen stone positioned to the right of the burial mound's entrance. She would link the phenomenon to her irrational belief in reincarnation when it was only his misfiring neurons.

"I've always loved it up here: makes me feel … comfortable."

The uncanny timing of the comment was typical Anna. One day, he would discover a logical explanation for it.

"Not much to draw with the mist and all, though."

"Hopefully it won't last long, Rich."

"So, forgetting the folklore and Rufus McJuggus or whatever his name is, what's the real history of the place?"

She halted the search for her pencils and frowned. "You better believe in magic by the time we have children, is all I can say."

"*If* I have any children, I'll be teaching him to question, observe and analyse."

"Him?"

There wasn't a need to have children present in him like there was in Anna. She may have been the most maternal woman he knew and Richard included his own mother in that list. But he already had a child, or rather he had always imagined he had one. Buried deep in Richard's mind like a memory, he could see the maturing features and wondering eyes of a small boy; a boy that he always saw when he considered his life and dreams. He may have been wrong but Richard had reasoned that the boy was really him. His late father often said he had never felt a day over twenty-one; maybe, at

twenty-seven, Richard still had the hunger of a nine year old.

"Him?" she repeated.

"I'll leave the magic to you. But please, no superstition."

She twisted her lips into a scrunch and resumed the pencil hunt while Richard remained wrestling possibilities. Maybe he was just plain scared to have children. What then? No children? He could not imagine being without Anna.

With his step heavier than before, he left his girlfriend and walked to the far end of the barrow, searching the peculiarly familiar landscape one more time in the hope of recalling some memory before descending into the mist.

It was probably both the instant chill that came with his descent and the growing sense of isolation that made him bury his hands in his pockets and cause his shoulders to huddle. By his side, poppies spattered the barrow like blood spots, and his vision was limited to several steps where cornflowers drooped sadly, their colours diminished by the grey cloak of the mist. He felt the pungent smell of the earth, roused by that moisture, prickle his nostrils. The same earth which seemed to have absorbed every heavy, sodden sound before they reached Richard's ears, making the enclosure he now inhabited feel utterly solitary.

Sometimes, having a compulsion to question agitated him. He was doing it now and his thoughts had adopted the gloom of the surrounding shroud. If he was scared to have a family, did that mean he was frightened of growing up? After all, he had done that already. He was an adult with a good job, or rather with a good firm. That had to mean something. He took care of himself … mostly. The family was the next step. But a family is for life, not just for Christmas, he added automatically.

There were two shapes were forming in the mist ahead. Perhaps it was because he was standing next to an ancient burial site, or maybe it was that mood of his, but they reminded him of gravestones. As the shapes emerged they darkened to the shade of thunder clouds and he could make out a sheen of fur, fluid over compact muscle, and two pairs of amber eyes watching him, and Richard realised they were just a couple of dogs. There was no noise from an approaching owner; no sound other than their panting. They had just appeared like phantoms into his, up until now, silent world.

Darwin, a black Labrador that slept on Richard's feet when he was a kid, guarded his dreams by keeping the monsters trapped under the bed or in the wardrobe. Darwin was a black Labrador. These weren't Labradors. They were hounds: hunting dogs.

A slobber-coated ball was released from the jaws of one of them. Its tongue lazily slapped against its muzzle whilst looking expectantly at Richard, offering an encouraging nod when the toy came to rest at his feet. He stopped short of picking it up when realising the object wasn't a ball at all, but a human skull. The dog gave a sharp whine, alternating his gaze between man and bone.

The cold penetrated his marrow and he shivered, wishing somebody, anybody, was in there with him. His search of the mist wall was not only to find the explanation for such a gruesome incident, but to seek reassurance that he was not alone. Neither were there.

"Wh …where did you get this, boy?" The words sounded as if they had sunk straight to his feet.

"Anna?" He called louder, turning in the direction he believed the burial chamber entrance to be, willing his voice to penetrate the silence, but the word slapped the ground like a sopping flannel. This forced muteness in the saturated confines only increasing his isolation.

The need for fresh air drove him up the side of the barrow. More from anxiety than in farewell, he threw the hounds and their plaything one last look, only to find that the dogs had disappeared. The skull, however, had not, and part of Richard argued to take the skull with him. It must be valuable in an archaeological sense; he tried not to think that it may be useful in a criminal investigation. Another part was asking why he didn't pick the bloody thing up. It was just a skull, after all. Just ...remains, even though it was leering at him.

He was halfway to the top and still within the mist, when he felt something cold and wet wriggle in his hand.

"Ugh!" He jerked his arm away.

A boy not much older than nine was standing on the slope next to him, holding out his hand. A roughly woven tunic, the hem of which reached his knees, appeared to be the only item that clothed him. Richard recognised him: it was the boy he had always imagined when he thought about his own past and future.

As if he had done it a thousand times before, Richard opened his palm and wrapped his fingers round the fragile bones of the boy's hand, taking the chill from the flesh. Upon this delicate contact, a single feeling surged from his chest to his toes, to his fingertips, to his scalp, shrivelling his anxieties, straightening his back and raising his chin. Pride.

Seeing that the boy's grimy, overcast face had been chased away by a sun shining from the wondering eyes, he was unable to do anything but grin brilliantly.

Hand in hand, they climbed out of the mist.

The warmth of a summer's morning greeted them. So did the fact that Richard had walked the opposite way to what he had thought and had surfaced at the far end of the barrow. On the entrance stone in the distance there was a woman sitting cross-legged. She appeared to be drawing. Despite her frequent looks in their direction, she showed no sign of having seen them. Neither did he make any attempt to attract her attention. Content with only the boy's company, he hoped the two of them would remain unnoticed.

However, they weren't to be alone for much longer he realised as the boy reached into the shifting veil of mist. A slender arm became visible, extending upward toward them. As its bony hand straightened, Richard could see the dashes, dots and solidus tattooed between knuckles and wrist that read 'I am'. The importance of this was brief and faded when the boy pulled the figure free of the mist. The link, through the child, with this woman enabled memories, trapped within the organic mesh somewhere at his core, to spark; memories of the three of them, a family, living here hundreds, thousands of years ago. He knew then that the woman had been his partner and the boy's mother. Had he always known, but not wanted to believe and always tried to disprove, that the boy who had remained with him in his head for a lifetime was his son? The realisation caused a knot to form in his throat. He could have broken down there and then, and if his son hadn't been by his side he would have done.

The little hand in his squeezed tight. Meeting the glittering blue eyes, it occurred to Richard that the boy had spent all those millennia wishing for this reunion.

Richard smiled back at the lad, then at the mother. Once, she had stood almost as tall as him, but her head was missing now. Its absence stirred neither repulsion nor fear only a vague sadness, and he wondered briefly if the skull that the hound had dropped once belonged to her, then they started walking. Swinging their child by his arms, the thought along with his indistinct unhappiness disappeared completely and was replaced by the sense of home for the second time that morning. Home with a son who he knew lay awake at night silent and stiff with fear, listening to animals close-by; whose favourite game was jumping on Richard's back to 'wrestle the bear'; who disliked the taste of the abundant blackberry. Home with a woman who, on her left thigh below the furs and woollen wrap, had the scars from a wolf bite.

Nearing the entrance, he surveyed the familiar hills to the soundtrack of his son's laughter, not remembering wanting anything to last more than this feeling of belonging. Richard and his son had found each other at last.

"And, I'll stay with you." The thought was out of his mouth before he knew it.

The brightness of that boy's smile now challenged the sun overhead. Convinced nothing would change how he felt, Richard nodded, giving the little hand, so breakable in his, the firmness of reassurance.

To his left, pages of a drawing pad flapped like an injured bird, and a pencil rolled then clattered as it struck the ground.

The chill of the stagnant mist had reached him, countering the heat of the bleeding sun as the mother led them, single file, down the treacherously-smooth stone steps toward the entrance of the barrow and rounded into a gloomy antechamber; a place which was fragrant with the rocks' mustiness, the sweetness of the earth and its rot. A dark place, save for a dim light in the furthest burial chamber illuminating the cracks and gaps between the hewn stone where dead poppies were scattered, their limp petals spreading like splashes; where rosemary sprigs tied with ribbons crawled with bugs; puddles of hardened wax stretched down over the natural ledges; and a woman was standing in the centre of the shrine holding her mobile phone aloft.

Her proximity jolted Richard.

"Anna?" He was almost sure that was her name, though she did not respond to his voice. The sense of frustration upon viewing her face and not placing it was akin to being a bug stranded on its back and frantically kicking in order to right itself before exhaustion. The strange urge to move nearer to her, to touch her, could not be achieved without breaking the link with his boy. So he remained several feet away, his thoughts struggling, scrabbling to grasp his past as he watched his lover, the mother of his child, approach the figure who so disturbed him.

Not only the build of the two women, but also the flat-footed way in which they walked was the same. Facing her, the mother raised a hand to touch the other's cheek. The caresses were lingeringly covetous ... and evocative: he had stroked those cheeks in much the same manner!

With the touches came more memories; a flurry, each doing a playful dance round his brain ... *living together in a dingy apartment with Anna for four years* ... he jumped for a memory ... *she painted* ... catching them between his fingers ... *sold her art online* ... placing each in a mental pocket ... *not for enough money, he had secretly thought ... her favourite animal was a cow ... she fantasized about buttered parsnips ... they had plans to start a family.*

As he collected them, his contentment began to seep from his pores like sweat and drip onto the cold floor of the chamber. Too many memories for him to grasp, no longer twirling, but buffeted head over heels like leaves kicked up by October gusts until finally, gladly, settling on the puddles of his contentment, soaking up the joy he had felt moments ago.

Remaining at his son's side, he saw his past and present coupled. The dried bloody neck topping the mother's thin decapitated body reminded him of the open tube of Old Holland's Red Ochre oil paint he had seen next to one of Anna's canvases recently. Her withering hands holding a face that was blooming even in the shadows that were closing in on him; a face radiant amongst laments cradled in dying flowers and impotent wishes presented as once-fragrant tributes.

Anna turned to face the daylight that for Richard seemed many miles away. He was standing in a mass grave, holding hands with the past, while his future was about to leave him behind.

This was not his life! This wasn't life.

"Anna!"

He glanced at his son. The once-wondering eyes of his son filled with a hope that was about to take a last gasp against a rising wave of crushing certainty. "I cannot stay."

Old enough to be ashamed by tears, his son could only squeeze his hand. The pressure of it seemed to constrict Richard's heart.

The bark of a dog, sharp and resounding, struck him. It was quickly replaced by a hollow knocking, rhythmless and eerie and as clear as the heartbeat in his ears. There was movement in the right burial chamber. Dirty-grey and mud coloured shapes dangling at waist-height became visible: skulls that were decorations attached to a macabre belt, the owner of which had yet to appear.

Deaf to the grisly cranial rattling, Anna lit one of the squat candles stuck in a puddle of hardened wax and turned off her phone light. The growing flame revealed what she could not feel: the mother standing behind her, her fingers clenching Anna's arms.

"To Ruckus Mogunt, King of the Hill, whoever you are," Anna said, placing a pencil next to the candle.

The skulls halted. A low growl intimidated the silence. To Richards's initial relief, the mother's response was to relinquish her hold, but Anna was approaching the mist hanging about the exit to the barrow.

"Anna, wait."

She did not, and she left him there alone.

His throat was brimming with a froth of reasons, logic, excuses, apologies, but his lips denied them exit, even when he untied his hand from the knot of flesh and saw what little still shone in his boy's eyes, shatter.

Richard looked to the exit. The way out was blocked by the sarsen stone.

"No!" He flung himself against the huge rock. "Anna!"

The cold, hard lump did not shift under his exertions, nor did his shouts cover the return of the knocking sound. Ruckus Mogunt was coming to ensure that Richard would never leave, that he would live in a house of bones with the woman without a head, and a boy that would never become a man.

His brain grasped at the image of Anna's pencil and he dug deep into his coat pockets searching for anything to appease the King of the Hill. A chewing gum wrapper, receipts, a length of string, hardened crumbs, grains of sand. In his trousers: a comb, his wallet, spare change.

"Have my watch! It's worth a mint." Was it worth his life? he thought. His shaking hands fumbled with the strap, unable to get the heavy item of jewellery off his wrist quickly enough.

The skulls were smirking at him as he thrust out the watch in his hand. The wearer of the skull girdle grew in the shadows of the steady flame. A furless bear decorated by a midnight sky of whorls and finger-lines.

"Take my watch," Richard said, "I don't belong here."

The face, cast gruesome in the glimmering firelight, was ingrained with dirt, and his braided whiskers hung the length of his bare chest like an anchor line. Was that sound of rain soaking into the earth, trickling through a myriad of routes round buried rubble and lost possessions to refresh the worms and beetles, the King's voice?

Struggling to leash his fear, Richard threw the offering to the floor. "It … it tells the time. It's yours."

The skulls rattled with a mirth that bounced against the chamber walls. In the morbid silence that followed, he saw the mother standing impassive in the reverent candlelight, felt his son's confusion writhe in his own belly, and heard a rapid flutter of wings drowned by an urgent chirruping.

His darting eyes frantically searched the grave until he found the source of the noise. There it was! A swallow on a ledge just inside the entrance.

Gone.

A grunt was belched from the throat of the king as they both saw how the bird had flown clear through the heavy sarsen stone blocking the escape.

Richard ran. He could almost feel wings spreading on his back as he asked himself how he could possibly be running through solid rock. When he fell into a sudden glare of sunlight he laughed aloud.

A little way from the barrow, where he lay, Anna was crouching by his side. "What's wrong? Where did you get to?"

He daren't open his mouth for fear he would vomit his heart. But then he saw what was leering at him from the insides of her bag.

"Wh … where did you get that thing?" he stumbled, scraping some distance between him and the skull.

"Isn't it amazing? I found it in the grass while I was searching for you."

He staggered to his feet.

"Where are you going?" she called after him.

He shook his head. "I don't know."

"Wait for me, then."

Richard left behind the grave and the King of the Hill. He managed not to look back until he was at the car and when he did the silhouette of his son keeping vigil was crowning the long barrow. A reminder of magic … and betrayal.

About The Author

Eric Nash, writer of Speculative fiction, has discovered that he enjoys editing and is looking to attend a self-help group to address this. His short fiction has been published in various excellent anthologies and magazines. You can catch up with him blog, at www.eanash.wordpress.com, or you can say hello at www.facebook.com/ericnashauthor and https://twitter.com/EANash1

TALE OF
THE WATER THIEF

BY SHAUN KILGORE

The trees themselves were gasping in the sweltering heat, struggling in the soaring temperatures that were already withering the fruit in the boughs. The creatures of the jungle were huddled in their burrows below the earth, blindly seeking a cool patch of earth to root in and protect them from the heat. The birds gave up their songs and the unlucky ones fell from their perches. The land was crying out for the sacred rains to come again. Drought had scorched the open lands to the north and the scourge moved to attack the deeper jungle. Neither prayer nor incantation seemed effective. The spirits were growing restless.

Half buried in a hovel of mud and reeds beneath a vine-choked tree, Sazu panted heavily. He dared not touch the water again. His last drink needed to last. The lack of rain lowered the Cancha River down to the bottom. The only water to be found for many miles was what one could scavenge from the spongy pulp of the dantuaga trees.

Sazu spent three days cutting swaths of the watery wood away and wringing the excess into a water pouch. Now he had enough water to last him two or three days.

The sky was bereft of any clouds and the swollen orb of the sun bore down on the jungle, making most activity too dangerous during the daylight hours. Sazu rested below the ground just like his animal brothers. When darkness fell, there was only a slight relief from the humidity. He had ventured from his den, pouch strapped to his back, corked to keep the precious water from leaking out. The wait was almost too much. Unable to see in the hovel, Sazu was forced to endure the sensations of worms and other creatures crawling around him, seeking the moisture. They writhed over his body. He tamped down the urge to cry out until the beasties moved on.

Sazu had difficulty gauging the passage of time below the earth. He was never sure until he removed the top of

103

his latest shelter whether darkness or sunlight would greet him. He longed to rove the jungle lands of his childhood, but to see it slowly dying was enough to hold him down until night had fallen.

On that day, he waited extra long. When Sazu emerged from the hovel, the jungle was still. A terrible portent to a realm once alive with the crying and chattering of dozens of creatures. Where had they all gone? Was he finally alone in the jungle?

It took a few moments for him to really see after the deeper darkness of the earth. The jungle floor was illuminated by moonlight, which was diffused by the thick growth of the trees. It seemed bright enough to Sazu though. He reached back into the hovel and retrieved his water pouch and his bow. The quiver he draped across the opposite shoulder. He moved away and padded across the detritus of dried out leaves and other things that squished between his bare toes. Sazu was grateful his sight wasn't that good. He was sure he didn't wanted to see what it was he was stepping on. The smell of decay and death told him enough.

Sazu kept a measured pace, always keeping his senses trained for even the slightest noise—not too hard to do in the unnatural silence of the jungle. He found himself praying to the gods of his people, the Mengagu. Yet there were no comforting words from the sacred ones who now looked on as the strange droughts pressed down on the land. A twinge of bitter feeling filled his heart. Sazu ceased praying in case the gods took offense. He didn't need the wrath of Oranth or Telashu poured out on his head. The Mengagu warrior was seeking an end to trouble not the beginning.

The undergrowth was still dense and Sazu spent more time picking his way through the breaks in the vegetation, taking his time so he would not disturb a hive of bees or get tangled in the coils of a great serpent. He kept looked around, his eyes squinted deeply to make out any shape or movement. The smell of death was sporadic. Sazu found the rotting corpes of the smaller creatures that made the forest floor their home. Occasionally, he made out the shape of a dead monkey. The Mengagu tried to avoid them as much he could. With so many littering the ground, there were bound to be panthers lurking in the shadows too.

After some time on the move, Sazu paused and unstopped the cap on his pouch. The water inside was warmer than he would have liked but the moisture felt wonderful on his dried lips and parched tongue. He found a tree to rest next to, but only gave himself a few moments before he was walking again. His travels by night were getting him further away from the heart of the jungle. It had been more than a week since he had been in familiar country. The land of his people was behind him. The path Sazu walked was a solitary one but he had known this when he had taken the charge from Rezi'Naven, the shaman. The wise man blessed him before all the Mengagu and sent him out based on a vision sent from the gods.

Sazu wondered which god had sent the dream to Rezi'Naven. Why did they demand he venture to edge of the jungle? No Mengagu had set foot beyond the sheltering trees of the Orakandi in living memory. The only thing the old shaman would say was that the gods had the waters of life, the living streams that would restore the land and those that dwelled upon it.

Tanuk, Sazu's father, had given him his best bow once it was clear that Sazu had been chosen by the gods. His mother packed the fruits and tubers he would need to sustain himself for the long journey across the jungle. *Food they could hardly spare*, Sazu remembered.

Sazu hefted the bow now, feeling the strength of the yew wood. The string he carried in a small pouch at his waist. The feel of the weapon was reassuring though he couldn't really use it in the darkness. With his other hand, Sazu kept the pouch from jostling about too much. Still, the water sloshed with each careful step. He needed to hear the jungle. He had this implacable feeling that he was being stalked by *something.* He didn't know what. The only noise was his feet rustling the leaves.

Sazu kept moving for hours in the warm night, his body covered in a sheen of sweat and his mouth drier than he would have liked. At some point, midway through his nighttime march, the Mengagu entered a slight clearing in the trees. The sky was revealed and the full glow of the moon penetrated to the jungle floor. It was the clearest view he had had in some time. Sazu stopped halfway across and sat on the ground. He unstopped the water pouch, drank deeply once, and replaced the cap. Next he removed some of the dried bananas and kiwi and ate. The meal was short and Sazu did not feel satisfied, but he didn't think he would have much luck hunting for meat. No time for a fire either.

I must move on. I cannot stop until I find it.

Sazu wasn't sure what <u>it</u> was, but he knew that he must reach the edge of the Orakandi. He believed that the gods would show him the way. *Why else would Rezi'Naven send me away?*

A twig snapped off to the right beneath the canopy.

Sazu jerked his head toward the sound and scanned the murky shadows. There was nothing that he could detect. His hands were fumbling with the pouch that contained his bowstring, even while eye gaze roved around. There were no other sounds. Sazu hurriedly strung the bow and drew an arrow from the quiver. He waited and listened. Nothing. Not even the sound of leaves rustling. His body was tense with anticipation. Whatever waited was gauging him. Seeing what sort of prey he was. Sazu struggled to keep his breathing in check, letting the air in and out of his lungs slowly and steadily. The hair stood up on the back his neck.

It was the only warning he had.

The black shape exploded out of the jungle from the opposite side. Sazu twisted his body around while he pushed himself away from the panther. In one smooth motion he loosed the arrow from the bow. The shaft flew true and jammed into the big cat's throat. There was a growl of pain but the beast went down just a pace short of Sazu. The black shape of it did not move. He waited for a few moments until his heart slowed. Sazu got up and went to the dead cat, gazing down on it in the moonlight, straining to see it. The beast seemed smaller. When he reached out he noticed how gaunt it was; starvation had worn away the fat and muscle. Sazu ran his fingers across the panther's ribs, which were visible even in the weak light.

"I do not fault you for trying to survive, brother panther. I pray you find good hunting in the great lands beyond." Sazu patted it again. He sighed and pulled the arrow out of the panther's ruined throat. He stooped down and brushed away the blood and flesh from the head and replaced it in the quiver.

Collecting his things, Sazu left the clearing behind. The panther remained where it was so the land could reclaim it. He moved easily in the jungle, walking briskly but not running. Sazu wanted to fly out of the Orakandi like the colorful peraki birds. His feet would have to carry him, but his heavenly thoughts bore him along steadily for the remaining hours of the night.

The first hints of dawn pulled him up short as the heat in the jungle became more unbearable with every step. Sweat poured from his brow and his body was drenched with it. Sazu was exhausted. He slowed down scanning the trees around him, and looking for just the right one. The earth was loose at its base. He came up and started rooting around in the dirt. The winding roots created pockets in the soil that could easily give way to create another shelter. Once he found one of these pockets and slid down into the earth, he took twigs and found strands of the thin, rope-like vines that wrapped around the tree trunk and wove together a cover for his shelter. It took another hour to finish. The heat pressed down on him, weakening him further. Sazu squinted as the first rays of the sun penetrated the treetops. He went down into the hole and covered himself. Beneath the surface, the ground was cooler. The soil soothed Sazu. Even though it was dark, he was able to adjust himself enough to take another drink before settling in to sleep. His weariness slid over him. And Sazu dreamed.

The shadows writhed in the half-light. Sazu jerked away from them and tried to make out his surroundings. It was a pit surrounded by gnarled roots that climbed the walls in a solid mass. The floor was smooth like river stone. Above, the branches of the trees interlocked into a canopy. Sazu glimpsed the sun through the gaps. Where he was below the earth, the air was moist and cool. No hint of the dry heat reached him.

A sharp intake of breath sounded in the space. Sazu spun around but he was alone. Then the steady rhythms of breathing flowed into the pit. There were no holes or openings to allow the air into the rough circle. Muttering voices rose up just at the limit of Sazu's hearing. He couldn't make out what they were saying. A chill pimpled his bare flesh.

The Mengagu realized he had no weapons.

His tongue stuck to the roof of his mouth. The voices became clearer—so clear in fact that Sazu realized there was more than one speaking. The bassy groans of male voices and the higher wavering trills of female voices mingled in discord. Sazu dropped to his knees and clamped his hands over his ears. So loud, so much pain.

"End the pain."

"Let the waters flow again."

"Come to us great waters."

"Let your blood sooth us, manchild."

Sazu shook his head, then pitched his voice higher. "I have been sent. I have been called by your brothers and sisters in the sky. The waters *will* flow again. Let me go!"

There was silence.

The stones shuddered beneath Sazu's feet, the ground rippled, and the walls of roots broke loose from the sides of the pit and reached out to grab at him. The rough surface of the roots scraped and scratched Sazu's skin. He pushed away and squeezed out of one branch only to be grappled by another. He was being crushed in the tangled mass. His cries were drowned out by the angry screams of the spirits of the earth. Blood flowed from his arms, legs, back, and belly.

"Stop it! Please stop. I only want to help!" Sazu's voice reverberated. The keening of the spirits crested and Sazu was wrapped in a dark embrace as the entire pit collapsed inward.

Sazu's screams were muffled. The next moment, he shoved upward and cast away the lid on his shelter and leapt out into the open. The jungle retained its unnatural quiet. Only a few scattered birds darted back and forth among the vine-choked trees. His eyes burned in the bright sunlight. He gasped as the hot air struck him.

Sazu battled to regain his senses. *Just a dream. Or maybe a vision.*

He sprawled on the grass, choking and sobbing. He didn't move. Couldn't move if he tried. His body was a mass of bruises and scrapes. For a time, Sazu just rested there, ignoring the fiery daytime temperatures that were slowly baking the jungle, maybe the whole world. Mengagu kept his eyes closed and images from the pit came back to him, the sounds of the spirits crying out echoed in his memory.

The dream was real enough to leave marks on me, he thought. *I must find a way to bring back the waters.*

His voice was hoarse so he spoke in a whisper. "Did you see this, Rezi'Naven? Did you know the depths of their pain? More than the ways of nature. Darkness. An evil spirit holds back the rains. Is the answer truly to be found beyond the Orakandi?" Hot tears rolled down his nose and dribbled to the ground.

Sazu lay in the dead leaves until the nightmare's grip faded from his mind. His throat was raw from screaming. Slowly, he rose up and crawled to the edge of his shelter, careful not to irritate the scrapes on his body. Sazu reached down and retrieved his bow, the quiver, and pouch. His scant possessions in hand Sazu felt more secure. He removed the cap and drank deeply of the water, not carrying that he would have to spend a few hours collecting more water from the trees. Sazu was certain he would not be sleeping again so soon. Instead, he busied himself with the task and only when he was finished drawing water did he eat some of the tubers.

Sazu felt refreshed. The afternoon heat had retreated giving him a reprieve and the chance to travel by daylight again. He wouldn't pass it up. A trill of birdsong stopped him in his tracks before he even started through the undergrowth. The sound seemed strange after so many days. Sazu scanned the treetops for a sign of the bird, but there was no movement. *A mind plays tricks, Sazu. Maybe yours more than most.*

The memory of the sweet sound wasn't something Sazu wanted to dismiss. He took it as an omen that he was back on the right path. *Maybe the spirits of the earth believe what I said?*

He was walking again and kept his pace steady as he angled through the jungle. Giant ferns obscured the ground ahead but Sazu pushed through the withered fronds, stepping over rotten logs and moving around the deadly thorn bushes. He walked until his muscles burned with the effort, traveling down into small ravines and back up again, steering clear of the tree roots that stuck up out of the ground. Their gnarled forms reminded him of the clawing images from his dream.

The day receded until the patches of sky spied between the overlapping trees faded from pale blue to pink, to orange, then purple and darker blue. Twilight descended on the jungle. Sazu had made good progress but he was worn out. His legs wobbled and he fell down in a thick patch of soft grass. The fragrance of the earth was again reassuring. He did not bother with a shelter but fell asleep there in the open beneath the canopy of trees, his bow nearby with an arrow ready.

A tremendous crackling awoke Sazu. He bolted upright, grabbed his bow, and nocked the arrow. He scanned the clearing, turning around in a circle. The sound disturbed the jungle again. It was a terrible sound like the branches of the trees being torn away violently. Sazu listened. He tracked the treetops looking for the barest hint of movement. Nothing

changed. Taking shallow breaths, he started out. The noise did not repeat. Sazu moved through the undergrowth with extra caution.

A twig snapped.

Sazu wheeled around and drew back the bowstring.

"Who is there?"

No answer.

Great Ones protect me this day.

Sazu turned around and continued trekking northward. After an hour of so, he realized the trees were thinning out. The ground was rockier and his steps sent dust into the air so that he was caked in the pale dirt. He coughed as the dust tickled his throat and finally had to stop to take a sip from the water pouch.

The crackling erupted suddenly. Sazu choked on the water and sprayed it out of his mouth and nose. He jammed the cork back in and crouched. The noise was much louder. When it came again, Sazu though he could almost discern the direction from which it came. Somewhere east from that spot. He headed towards the sound determined to discover the source.

Maybe I'll find the answer I've been seeking. Sazu let the thought flicker in his mind as he descended a rocky hill. The air was getting drier as he headed towards the sound. The cracking repeated for several minutes, allowing him to trace it. He let his hunter's instincts guide him. A few hasty prayers to the gods and the spirits of the Orakandi were added for good measure. He even muttered a word to Rezi'Neven, hoping the shaman might hear him with his otherworldly means and give him a bit of wisdom to keep him alive.

Beyond the hill, he reentered the trees. The space between them had widened enough to let the relentless blaze of the sun pour down below the canopies to the brush gathered on the floor. Sazu was sweating now. The crackling cut off. At the last sounding, he glimpsed the tops of the trees furthest away shake and fall out of sight.

Whatever was making the sound was tearing at the trees. Sazu kept going even though the sun was reaching its crest so that it beamed down on his head. He unstopped the pouch and drank more of the water, but each sip was never enough to wash away the dry feeling.

The silence closed in around Sazu. The jungle was inert. The Mengagu traipsed through the dying boughs still heading in the general direction of the sound. He was closing in on the point where the trees fell. The light grew brighter until Sazu could see a clearing ahead. As he reached the last of the trees he had to squint to see through the blinding brightness of the sun. What he saw made his body quiver and tingle.

Scores of trees had been brought down. The landscape had been rent into pieces, the ground ripped up, roots of trees exposed. Then Sazu saw something he could not understand. Hundreds of yards away, he spied a tall, shining stalk that reflected the sun. It rose into the sky several feet and ended in a ball-like shape that glowed like the coals in a fire. Small rods extended from the main stalk at all angles, like branches on a tree. At the end of each one, a small ball glowed bluish white.

As he stared in awe, the stalk shuddered and stirred up the dust and withered leaves from the broken husks of the trees. Sazu then noticed a patch of dantuaga trees still intact on the opposite side. The smaller balls flickered in time with the larger one on the peak of the stalk. Then there was a hum that vibrated Sazu's entire body. The sensation was not pleasant. He struggled just to watch what happened. The glow extended like a bank of fog rolling across the wetlands.

Crack!

The dantuaga trees shattered and the moisture of the bark was sprayed everywhere. Then in an instant it was like some invisible hand had gathered the water and drew it together into a bubble. The whole batch floated through the air until it touched the stalk. Sazu noticed small holes opening on the shiny surface. The water was absorbed into them.

Sazu gasped, shaking his head in denial. "Blessed ones!"

The strange stalk took the water. Looking beyond the closest one, he searched the broken lands to the north. Despite the bright day, Sazu though he saw the shimmer of other stalks busy with their work.

"What are these beasts?"

Fear sent a chill through Sazu. He wasn't sure what to do next. Or if there was anything he could do.

I have to find out more. I need to learn what they are. Sazu clambered down amidst the debris and slowly moved towards the nearest stalk.

There was no easy path through the mess. Sazu had to climb up over the remains of trees with their roots splayed out, over piles of dirt that had been gouged out of the earth. As he traversed the field of debris, the stalk carried out its work and more dantuaga trees were drained of their moisture. As he crawled up over another mound, something new happened.

Near the base of the stalk, the rods closest to the ground dipped down, their bluish color shifting to lavender then red. Sazu was momentarily blinded by the flash then there was a rumbling sound that shook the earth be-neath him. Sazu grabbed for the roots of a tree and held on. When he could see, he saw that holes had been bored out by the rods. A stream of water was flowing upwards out of the ground. The holes on the stalk collected it the same way.

They're harvesting all the water from the land.

Sazu glanced up at the pulsing orb at the head of the stalk. There was a haze surrounding it.

The urge to drink was growing and Sazu tried to blink but it was painful. The sun blazed and poured more heat on the dry air. Suddenly, Sazu under-stood. "It drinks the water from the air too."

Sazu slipped down and sought shelter in the shade beneath the over-hanging roots. The crackling contin-ued. More trees died while he sat there helpless. The harvest did not slow or show any sign of weariness. The crack-ling was relentless. Sazu closed his eyes and tried to block out the awful sound. The dry air was making it hard-er to breathe and stay comfortable. His lips were shriveled and his throat was scratchy.

I have to do something. This is why I was sent.

Steeling himself, Sazu left the shel-tering roots and readied his bow. Once he was in position, he drew back the arrow, aimed for the stalk, and let loose. The shaft sailed through the sky, arching up and then down to strike the shiny stalk just below the top.

Ting!

The arrow struck with a strange, metallic sound and bounced harmlessly to the ground. Sazu shook his head. He drew another arrow and shot at the ball mounted atop the stalk. As he watched, the shaft dropped down on it and in a burst of light and flame, the arrow was burned to ash.

"Gods," Sazu gasped.

The light on the main ball changed, becoming touched with reds and violets. The smaller balls on the branches followed moments after. A low hum filled the air and the lights all began to pulse. Sazu's stomach twisted. There was something menacing about the change. He went tense and remained still, half hidden by the barrier of roots. The pulsing grew stronger, the hum deeper, until the sound was moving in time with the rapid throbbing of color. Sazu continued to walk, fixated by the light.

The high-pitched whine split the air. A loud booming sound like thunder followed. The ground not more than a dozen paces away exploded with a deafening roar. Sazu was pelted by the fragments of wood and dirt. His ears were ringing.

Not waiting for the next attack, Sazu ran away, bounding up and down the mounds of dirt. The whine pierced again. Fountains of dirt surged up to either side of him. Panic lent him speed and he raced as fast as his feet could bear him, collapsing once he'd returned to the edge of the jungle tree line.

He watched the creature return to its deadly work. The same was being repeated by others on the edge of Sazu's sight.

"I cannot do this alone. No one man can stop these beasts."

The orbs pulsed their steady rhythms, systematically working to draw in the moisture as they were made. The watery pulp of the trees contained what the rivers no longer supplied. Across the northern expanses of the once fertile country above the jungle called the Orakandi, the orbs with their long silver stalks and receptacle branches, carried on.

From the trees of the jungle, a thousand pairs of eyes watched, waited, and planned. The day came and it was an ordinary day. The Mengagu warriors rained down a storm of arrows and stones on the stalks prompting defensive responses from them. As explosions erupted on the ruined land, the warriors came at it from different directions, attacking, feigning, and then returning with ferocity.

Sazu screamed, bearing his teeth with his brothers, as they ran towards the base of the stalk. The branches flashed like lightning and bolts struck among them. Still, the Mengagu attacked. It was life or death. The jungle spirits cried out, the threat had been found, and the people of the Orakandi would fight until the end. Sazu caught a glimpse of the wily Rezi'Neven, spear held in grizzled hands, his eyes wide with the warrior's cry, before the light and heat consumed him.

About The Author

Shaun Kilgore is the author of various works of fantasy, science fiction, and a number of nonfiction works. He has also published numerous short stories and collection. His books appear in both print and ebook editions. Shaun is the publisher and editor of MYTHIC: A Quarterly Science Fiction & Fantasy Magazine. He lives in eastern Illinois. Visit www.shaunkilgore.com for more information.

Help us pay our authors better rates for their stories and make MYTHIC a better magazine.

Join us. Become part of the MYTHIC team. Consider supporting us monthly by becoming a Patron through *Patreon* and receive exclusive offers and other rewards.

For more information you can visit our page at:

www.patreon.com/mythicmag

The
Inter States
Series:

What if America failed to decisively turn away from fossil-fuel dependence when it still had the capital and geopolitical security to do so?

What if the disappearance of America's middle class became a permanent condition, and, along with it, the disappearance of national popular democracy in all by name only?

What if the effects of climate change started to significantly affect U.S. politics and economics?

"Crisp, fast-paced, and uncomfortably plausible....a new series set in a crumbling, dysfunctional United States in the not too distant future. Readers who want something more interesting and challenging than one more helping of yesterday's futures will find Meima's narrative well worth their time."

-John Michael Greer

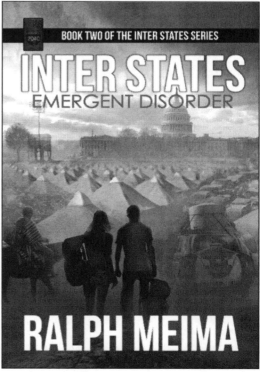

REVIEWS

'PRESS START TO PLAY'
EDITED BY DANIEL H. WILSON
AND JOHN JOSEPH ADAMS

REVIEWED BY STEPHEN REID CASE

Press Start to Play
Daniel H. Wilson
& John Joseph Adams, Editors
Vintage Books, 2015

I remember video games. I had a GameBoy once upon a time, convinced that it was the smarter choice because its portability meant I could take it camping with me on our annual family pilgrimages to northern Michigan.

Years later, stuck at home with low blood counts due to chemotherapy, my parents would rent me a Nintendo 64 and I'd wander the castle corridors for hours with Mario. In college, I played through the immersive MYST sequels, at least one of the Final Fantasy games (the one my roommates assured me was best), and the Soul Reaver series. I had a subscription to PCGamer for a year or two, though I appreciated it more for its design and beautiful gaming ads than because I was actually playing any of the games reviewed.

Despite this limited experience though, video games are a realm from which I've been absent for long time. I'm pretty far from being a gamer, and I'm even farther from agreeing with author Ernest Cline's claim in his forward to this volume of short stories that video games satisfy an important biological imperative for us to fight, search, hunt, and solve puzzles. What

I'm more interested in are a different set of questions this new anthology brings forward: do video games satisfy our needs not simply as clever apes deprived of the struggle for survival but rather our needs as human beings? That is, are they a viable means of telling new and important stories? *Can a video game be a piece of literature?*

This collection is a book of stories that are either about or in some way engage the medium of video games, but it's also a means at getting at some of the questions above. I think many of the authors included in this volume would argue that, yes, video games can be literature. Many of these authors are themselves writers for video games, and their work shows that some games at least go far beyond simply solving puzzles, finding treasure, and blowing things up. There is a lot of what you would expect in here: stories that play with the idea of games and gaming. Some of them do this very well, like the tongue-in-cheek fantasy "Save Me Plz" by David Barr Kirtley, which examines a fantasy RPG bleeding into reality. Others, such as "NPC" by Charles Yu and "GodMode" by Daniel H. Wilson, left me scratching my head, not because of any fault in the writing but because I apparently don't live deeply enough in the gaming paradigm to understand them.

Some of the stories here pushed into more "literary" territory— taking the concept of video games out of action-adventure tropes and using them as a scalpel to examine the hearts of people and relationships. Some of the luminously literary bits in here included "The Relive Box" by T. C. Boyle, which was terrifying and heartbreaking and utterly believable. It is a story about regret and nostalgia plugged into virtual reality while actual life crumbles around a father and the world he has left behind. "Coma Kings" by Jessica Barber follows a similar theme, playing with the idea of being lost to the real world, of abandoning it, for a game. The realistic piece "All of the People in Your Party Have Died" by Robin Wasserman is another along these lines, set in the 1980s and following a college graduate coming to terms with her sexuality and her loss of idealism through the lens of the text-based game *The Oregon Trail*.

The example of text-based games like *The Oregon Trail* provided some of the authors in this collection an ideal means to blend the lines between gaming and prose in their stories. The stories "1UP" by Holly Black and "Roguelike" by Marc Laidlaw do this well, but pieces like Ken Lui's "The Clockwork Soldier" takes this to another level, embedding a text-based game to create a nested narrative, a story within a story. As another example, "<end game>" by Chris Avellone, despite an ambiguous and unsatisfying ending, turns this convention on its head by telling the "real" bits of the story in game-like text while the "game" portion is given in vivid prose narrative.

Another batch of stories in this collection that stood out were those that played with the history and lore of video games themselves, exploring or inventing urban legends of early, hard-to-find games or the mysteries within games and hints of how to beat them scattered across the young days of the internet. *"Desert Walk"* by S. R. Mastrantone for instance, tells the story of a gaming historian trying to track down what might be the rarest game ever created and the grim secret it contains. Catherynne M. Valente's "Killswitch" is another, an atmospheric piece describing an enigmatic game that is almost itself a piece of poetry.

Finally, another type of story in this excellent collection that took me a bit by surprise were those that had a clear social message, either exploring the negative aspects of gaming or providing a plea to resist their allure and not abandon the real world for the screen. Some of these seemed a bit heavy-handed, despite the interesting concepts in some of them (such as "Anda's Game" by Cory Doctorow, about an MMOG in which labor issues become a reality). Chris Kluwe's "Please Continue" is perhaps the most curious of these, an appeal in the guise of a narrative,

though one with a message that fits the high quality of this collection. Personally, I thought Hugh Howey's "Select Character" was the smartest approach to social commentary through gaming, a story in which commentary on our war-mongering gaming culture is contrasted with ideals of care and cultivation as a woman steadily builds a virtual garden in her husband's war-torn first-person shooter.

It turns out that I don't know enough about gaming to know whether some video games can function as literature. But this collection shows that gaming, as a human experience common to many of us, can certainly be used as a lens with which to create literature. Moreover, the nature of the medium itself— at the intersection of the human-technology boundary— makes it particularly amenable for quality science fiction. If you are a gamer, were a gamer, or just enjoy good story telling using the pieces of technology around us today, this is a collection for you.

Available
From Founders House and Other Booksellers
in Trade and Electronic Editions

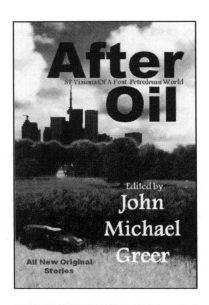

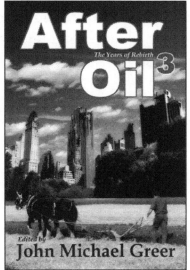

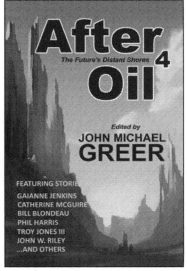

REVIEW
'RETROTOPIA'
BY JOHN MICHAEL GREER

REVIEWED BY FRANK KAMINSKI

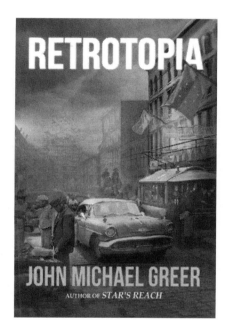

Retrotopia
John Michael Greer
Founders House Publishing,
December 2016,
254 pages, $15.99

With his novel *Retrotopia*, John Michael Greer seeks to challenge the perceptions most people have of technology. His aim is partly to spur aware-

ness about what "technology" actually is, since we're so used to seeing it equated with electronic gizmos that we tend to have a limited sense of it. (How many people realize that stone tools and study circles are every bit as much examples of technology as are computers?) On another level, Greer wants to make the point that individuals, as well as whole societies, can and do make conscious choices about which technologies they wish to use (the Amish being a particularly apt case in point). You need not own a TV, a car or a smartphone just because everyone says you should. By that same token, an entire nation need not follow the same technological path as the rest of the industrial world, especially when there's another, more sensible way.

Greer walks his talk on the issue of technological choice, having happily lived his entire adult life without a TV, an automobile or a mobile phone. Now he's attempting to use fiction to dispel some of the strangeness that still, in most people's minds, attends the notion of rejecting modern-day innovations in favor of things from the past. To do so is what Greer calls "retrovation," which, as its name suggests, is the opposite of innovation. Whereas the latter involves coming up with new technologies, the former consists of rediscovering old ones. For it happens that many past technologies are superior to their modern-day equivalents. It's often been the case that the inventions that won out did so not on their own merits, but because of sheer circumstance or the machinations of those with an interest in seeing them succeed. (Consider the General Motors streetcar conspiracy of the 1920s to '40s, which gave automobiles a monopoly on surface transportation in America.)

Greer's novel is about a future nation in what is now the American Midwest that has managed to prosper by going backwards technologically. It's 2065, and the United States long ago descended into civil war and dissolution as a result of having continued down the same shortsighted trajectory it's on today: namely, the pursuit of infinite growth on a finite globe. Most of the handful of post-U.S.A. American nations remain fixated on this unachievable goal. However, one country, the Lakeland Republic, has chosen

an alternate course. It has decided to discard the ideal of growth for its own sake as well as any technologies aimed at achieving that goal. From the perspectives of those in surrounding nations, an aura of mystery surrounds the goings-on in the Lakeland Republic. And first-time visitors often find that the mystery only deepens once they've set foot within the Republic's borders.

How can it be, they wonder, that this country is able to enjoy such prosperity and internal peace while embracing such counterintuitive policies? Unlike most other nations, the Republic refused to accept conditions laid out by the International Monetary Fund (IMF) and the World Bank for economic assistance following the war. As a result, it defaulted on its debt, lost access to world credit markets and had an international trade embargo imposed on it. Yet by nearly every measure, it's faring better than any other nation on the continent. It has none of the war wreckage that continues to litter other lands, its towns are in markedly better shape and its working class has such a high standard of living that a tide of hopeful immigrants pours in from elsewhere.

It turns out that the Republic became such a success story precisely because it chucked the conventional wisdom on how to rebuild a national industrial economy. The embargo, together with the Republic's decision to stop throwing good money after bad in terms of its debt, allowed capital to accumulate inside the country. Three decades later, the nation has succeeded in rebuilding its economy from the bottom up, taking care to avoid the follies that threw it into the abyss in the first place.

Retrotopia's plot concerns the journey, both physical and psychological, of a newcomer named Peter Carr. The neighboring country of the Atlantic Republic has just had a presidential election, and Carr is an advisor to the president-elect. In the novel's opening scene, he's traveling to the capitol of the Lakeland Republic, Toledo, where he is to spend the next two weeks helping draft a set of key agreements between the two governments. As Carr goes about his daily business in Toledo, we're provided a comprehensive tour of how things work in this bizarre new land.

From the moment he crosses over into Lakeland (via a 1950s-era diesel-electric locomotive run on used frying oil), Carr is dumbfounded by the seeming technological backwardness he encounters. He's horrified to learn that the country wants nothing to do with the metanet (this future's Internet) and uses jamming stations to keep out the satellite transmissions on which metanet access depends. Carr is also baffled by the chaotic technological

bricolage he observes everywhere. He sees farms worked by draft horses just as commonly as those boasting tractors. He also passes through city neighborhoods in which streets populated by cars and trucks exist right alongside those where horse-drawn carriages and streetcars predominate. And he sees much more in the way of handcrafted everyday goods than he's used to, an indication that the household economy has made a comeback here. What's more, the average Lakelander gives no more thought to the disparate technological choices others have made than most people today give to the supposed need to own a smartphone.

The Lakeland Republic is divided into counties, with each county free to fashion its own unique technological landscape. There's a tier system of technological development, with the highest tier, five, representing 1950s-era infrastructure; and the lowest, roughly that of the 1830s. A lower tier means a lower tax burden for the county's inhabitants, but also a more rudimentary infrastructure. The citizens of each county vote to determine which tier best suits their needs. This does not mean, however, that individual residents of a lower-tier county are prohibited from having higher-tier technologies if that's what they wish. On the contrary, they're quite able to do so–but they must pay out of their own pockets for the privilege. Because of this system, there's significant incentive for people to eschew the latest and greatest in favor of the ever-more-old-fashioned.

Over the course of the plot, Carr has a series of errands to run, each one bringing to light some new aspect to life in the Lakeland Republic. For the first time in his life he pays for things with checks and paper money, rather than electronically. When he tears one of his shoes and has to buy a replacement pair, he learns the difference between the shoddy plastic footwear he's accustomed to and the quality, hand-crafted shoes Lakelanders wear. He also falls ill for a couple of days, and in the process receives a lesson in how much better healthcare is in Lakeland than in the Atlantic Republic. (What he's used to is basically an even more extreme version of what Americans have today. Lakeland healthcare, in contrast, is all about affordability, access for all and the use of natural remedies rather than industrially produced pharmaceuticals.) And as Carr endeavors to keep up on current events, he has his first exposure to long-form print journalism, a far cry from the 140-character metanet articles he's used to reading.

Carr's visits to various cultural, economic and governmental establishments provide another means of introducing both him and us to the workings of the Lakeland Republic. His destinations include an energy plant, a public school, a library and a military outdoor shooting range. During his tour of the energy plant, he's impressed to learn of the enterprising scheme Lakelanders have developed for turning sewage into electrical power. While visiting the school, he gets to witness an education system focused not on preparing kids for meaningless standardized tests, but rather on teaching them how to think for themselves and directly apply what they've learned. The library's ambiance is disconcerting at first: "In place of the clatter of keys and the babble of voices that gave the libraries I knew their soundtrack," Carr recounts, "the room was as hushed as a funeral parlor." (I chuckled at this description, sensing that it was Greer's way of grumbling ironically about the sad state of the modern-day library experience.) As for Carr's time at the shooting range, it provides an eye-opening object lesson in the astonishing edge that antique weapons can have over the most state-of-the-art drones.

It's while visiting a streetcar factory that Carr sees perhaps the most poignant example yet of how radically different the rules of Lakelandian economics are from those of his country. During his tour, he notices that the production line workers are using hand tools rather than machines, prompting him to ask why the company hasn't automated its process. His tour guide is aghast at the suggestion. "If we tried to automate our assembly line, given the additional costs," she explains, "the other two firms would eat us alive." This is because the Lakeland Republic has laws that make it cost-ineffective to employ machines rather than people. These laws impose steep taxes on businesses that choose to automate, as a way of compensating the greater society for the resultant increases in unemployment and pollution. Such costs can no longer be written off as externalities.

One part of this book that I particularly admire is its satire directed against the existing order. In so many ways, Carr embodies how reliance on modern-day technology has dulled people's innate abilities. Like most people in America today, he depends on gadgets to carry out nearly every activity of daily life—and as a result, he struggles to do math in his head, write legibly and in general work with his hands. These deficiencies are brought into sharp relief during his time in the Lakeland Republic, where he suddenly has to write things down, do math without a calculator and track down books in a library.

My favorite thing about Retrotopia is the way it overlays modern progressive ideals onto a world of retro technology. Since the Lakeland Republic has traveled back in time technologically, one might assume it has also done so socially—yet this is not so. During his time there, Carr becomes involved in an intimate romantic relationship, witnesses a same-sex wedding and meets a prominent public figure with a spouse of the same sex. Thus, while Toledo may have 1950s technology, it has in no way returned to that era's social mores. Greer says he made it this way specifically to drive home the message that historical periods aren't indivisible units that must be accepted or rejected wholesale. In his experience, this point is lost on most people. "I've long since lost track of the number of times I've been told," he reports, "that rejecting the latest new, shiny, and dysfunctional technology, in favor of an older technology that works, is tantamount to cheerleading for infant mortality, or slavery, or living in caves, or what have you."[1]

Given its title, one obvious question many readers will have about *Retrotopia* is whether it's at least partly an homage to *Ecotopia*, one of the great eco-novels of the 1970s. The answer is that, yes, Greer deeply admires this seminal work by the late Ernest

[1] John Michael Greer, "A Time for Retrovation," *The Archdruid Report*, Sept. 21, 2016, https://thearchdruidreport.blogspot.de/2016/09/a-time-for-retrovation.html?commentPage=2 (accessed May 24, 2017).

Callenbach, and he includes nods to it in his own tale. Most crucially, both books use the device of a first-person narrator with whom the reader is meant to identify. In *Ecotopia*, this character is a journalist rather than a government official, but he serves exactly the same function as does Mr. Carr: to provide readers an up-close, outsider's view of an unfamiliar world. Another similarity is how meticulously realized both books' settings are. Greer and Callenbach both go into such detail that it's as if they're describing real places.

Yet there are also some notable departures from Ecotopia. The most important of these has to do with Greer's concept of retrovation. The appeal of retrovation seems to have been lost on Callenbach, since he saw future technological advances–for example, improvements in solar photovoltaics and other renewable energy technologies–as having the potential to rescue us from our impending energy descent. Greer, who is nothing if not a realist, sees no such potential. In short, Callenbach maintained his faith in innovation, whereas Greer sees continued innovation as the exact opposite of what's needed, hence the Lakeland Republic's decision to look to the past for workable answers to humankind's crises.

Another big difference between *Ecotopia* and *Retrotopia* lies in their differing character arcs. *Ecotopia's* main character comes full circle, abandoning his life back home to become an Ecotopian. Without giving anything away, I'm happy to say that this isn't the choice Greer makes for his character. Greer decides instead to take things in a less predictable, more ambiguous—and more interesting— direction, in keeping with his view that there isn't one be-all-and-end-all response to the challenges before us.

This book is yet another solid entry in the oeuvre of a profoundly accomplished author. In writing it, Greer drew on his encyclopedic knowledge of history and a wide range of other fields to create a fully realized, believable world that deftly turns the assumptions of present-day industrial society on their ears. While I don't have any major complaints about the job he's done, I did find myself yearning for more detail on some of the other post-U.S.A. nations besides the Lakeland Republic. However, since Greer's main purpose is to show us a portrait of the Lakeland Republic, this isn't so much a criticism as a testament to how thoroughly he drew me into his fictional world.

Made in the USA
Columbia, SC
11 July 2017